# GLENROE
# THE BOOK

## MICHAEL JUDGE

*stories from the RTE series created by Wesley Burrowes*

Gill and Macmillan
and
Radio Telefís Éireann

Published by
Gill and Macmillan Ltd
Goldenbridge
Dublin 8
and
Radio Telefís Éireann
Donnybrook
Dublin 4
© Michael Judge 1990
0 7171 1786 3
Typeset by
Seton Music Graphics Ltd, Bantry, Co. Cork
Printed by
Butler & Tanner Ltd, Somerset
Colour origination
Kulor Centre, Dublin

# CONTENTS

1.  The Blow-Ins     1

2.  The MacDermott Story     17

3.  Market Forces     33

4.  Que Sera Sera     41

5.  The Rocky Road to Rome     67

6.  Going to the Dogs     85

7.  The Big House     109

8.  For Worse or Better     121

9.  Michelle     137

10. Teasy's Men     156

11. Even Stephen     175

# • CHAPTER ONE •

# THE BLOW-INS

Biddy MacDermott came into the kitchen carrying an armful of logs and kicked the door shut behind her. Small and neat (*compact* was the word she liked to use about herself) she was dressed in a loose sweater and jeans, in contrast to her mother, who was standing in front of the mirror, making a final inspection of her face. Mary MacDermott, at forty-three, had all the sartorial smartness lacking in her twenty-three-year old daughter, from the top of her expertly coiffured head to the high heels which set off her slim and elegant legs. She had kept her good looks and figure by constant attention, careful cultivation and a determination not to let the life of a farmer's wife age her prematurely, as she had seen it do to so many of her neighbours.

Biddy dropped her load of logs into the basket beside the fire and looked her mother up and down.

'Going out?'

'Mm. How do I look?'

'Bridge, is it?'

'Yes.'

Biddy grinned.

'For bridge you look OK.'

Mary adjusted her chic little hat and shrugged herself into her grey woollen coat.

'What does that mean?'

'Well,' said Biddy, 'I don't imagine your bridge cronies are going to be inspecting you very closely. Now, if you were going on a date....'

Mary shot a glance at her daughter, but Biddy had plumped herself down in an easy-chair and picked up a magazine, apparently quite unconscious of any implications in her words.

'What's wrong with me?' asked Mary.

'Not a thing in the world.'

'You're sure?' Mary had another look at herself in the mirror. 'Some of those old harpies down in the Club study more than the cards.'

'Mam, you're beautiful,' said Biddy. 'And you get more beautiful the older you get.' She paused a moment, then said deliberately, 'Any man's fancy.'

1

Mary took the compliment, but disregarded the addendum. Arguments always tired her.

'Well, I'm off. Supper's all ready in the oven. You just have to serve it.'

'Are you not having any?'

'I haven't the time,' said Mary. 'As a matter of fact, I'm late already.'

'You're a slave to the bridge, Mam.'

'Oh you know the way it is,' said Mary, ignoring the trace of irony in Biddy's voice. 'They come to depend on you and you just can't let them down. Especially not tonight.'

'I've heard that before.'

'No, really. The President's Prize is next week and we're all practising like mad.'

'Yeah.'

There was another pause and for a moment their eyes met. Mary coloured slightly under her daughter's direct gaze and she turned away, picking up her gloves and handbag from the table.

Biddy said, 'There was somebody looking at the Hill farm today.'

'Was there?' Mary was glad at the change of subject. 'Was Dick Moran with him?'

'No. Matt.'

'Time for it to go,' said Mary. 'They've had it on their hands long enough.'

'We could have taken it. It's not as if we hadn't the money.'

'Sure, haven't we enough already,' said Mary. 'More than your father and yourself can manage. What was he like?'

'Who?'

'The man who came to look. I presume it was a man?'

Biddy said, 'It was a man all right.'

Mary paused in the doorway.

'Well?'

'Well what?'

'Was he tall or short or young or old or what was he?'

'He wasn't old,' said Biddy.

'Well, that's something,' said Mary, smiling at her.

'He looked a bit of a gom,' said Biddy, opening the magazine and beginning to study the television programmes.

Mary studied her daughter a moment. 'You might think of getting your hair done.'

Biddy made a grimace. 'Mam . . .'

'Forget I said it. You'll be all right getting the supper?'

'Amn't I always all right!' said Biddy.

When she heard her mother's car drive away, Biddy closed the magazine. She rose from her chair and stood in front of the mirror. Instead of Mary's thin face, she saw her own round one. Instead of her mother's well-groomed hair, she saw her own untidy mop. Instead of the 'little black number' her mother wore, she saw her own sweater and jeans. She made a face at herself. Well, it was her own life, her own decision. Looking after the thirty-five acres of the farm devoted to tillage — her father confined his attention to the cattle — left her precious little time to be dolling herself up like her mother. Anyway, she wasn't very much given to socialising. She had spent so much of her life convincing the farmers around her that she was their equal in every way and should be accepted as such that she scorned to use the usual female tricks of personal adornment in order to impress people. They could take her as she was, sweater and wellies and all, or they could do the other thing.

And anyway there was the shyness, the dreadful confusion which always overcame her when she was required to put on a dress and join what she called the chorus-line at dances.

'You're hopeless, Biddy Macdermott,' she said to her reflection in the mirror.

Her father came into the kitchen. Michael MacDermott was in his seventies, a white-haired, monosyllabic man who went about his farming duties in complete silence and who rarely spoke even in the intimacy of his own home.

'Was that your mother?' he asked.

'You just missed her,' said Biddy. 'She's gone to play bridge. But you needn't worry — I'll have your supper on the table in a couple of minutes.'

Michael nodded and left the room again.

'Don't go too far away,' Biddy called after him. 'I really mean a couple of minutes.'

There was no answer.

As she busied herself setting the table for the meal, Biddy thought again about the man who was interested in buying the Hill farm.

'There's two of them,' Matt Moran had volunteered, when she called him over after the client had gone. 'Father and son.'

'Which was that?'

'Ah for God's sake, Biddy, that was the son!'

'I only asked,' said Biddy. 'He looked a bit . . . sort of craggy about the face.'

'Miley's all right,' said Matt.

'D'you know him well?'

'You're very interested, aren't you?' Matt grinned at her.

'Don't be an eejit, Matt.' Biddy grinned in her turn. 'I'm interested in anybody who's going to be living in my ear. What's he like?'

'I've only met him a couple of times at Macra dances,' said Matt. 'A bit of a slob in some ways. You know, shy. Hasn't a lot to say for himself.'

'Not like one of the fast-talking Morans.'

'You've got it in one.'

'How old is he?'

'I don't know. Thirties somewhere. It's very hard to tell with Miley. Too old for you, anyway.'

Biddy said deliberately, 'How do you know I don't take after my mother? You know, go for the older man.'

Matt looked at her. He had stopped smiling. 'I suppose stranger things have happened.'

They both avoided the delicate subject of Biddy's mother and Matt's father, Dick Moran.

'Where does he come from?'

'They were farming sheep above at Slievebracken.'

'Mountainy men!'

'Now you're talking like Paddy Maher,' said Matt. 'The first thing he said to me, in fact. "Blooming Byrnes coming down from the mountains and taking over the lowlands." And Slievebracken really only up the road! Of course, anything south of Carmody's farm is Indian country to Paddy.'

'They won't be rearing sheep here, will they?'

'I couldn't care if they were rearing camels, as long as the deal goes through.'

'You think it won't?

'The father is dragging his feet,' said Matt. 'He has the few bob in his pocket from the sale of Slievebracken and he likes the feeling. But Miley is anxious to buy. Otherwise he's threatening to go off to England.'

Biddy remembered again the tall man in the blue anorak she had seen walking the Hill farm with Matt that afternoon. A big awkward man with a calm expression on his weather-lined face, he had towered above young Matt, who had still not managed to achieve the effect of confident maturity necessary to his profession as auctioneer and who smiled too much in an effort to make up for his deficiencies. But Matt was under his father's thumb. Miley Byrne didn't appear to suffer from the same complaint, even if he looked a bit soft. She wondered what he would be like as a neighbour.

She hoped the deal would go through. For Matt's sake, she told herself. The Hill farm had been lying idle too long.

A week later Biddy knew that the sale had indeed taken place. From a distance she watched as a battered car towing an equally battered trailer rattled up the laneway and groaned to a stop in front of what had been the Regans' cottage. Both car and trailer were crammed with furniture and other belongings, all jumbled in together and tied down by various pieces of rope in a most inexpert fashion.

Two men got out of the car. One was the tall man she had seen with Matt Moran, the other was shorter and older. The older man wore a cap and walked with a decided limp. He stretched himself and looked about him and immediately spotted Biddy as she stood staring at them from beyond the fence. He raised his hand in greeting and she waved back, a little shamefaced at having been caught watching them. She was glad that the younger man had already gone into the cottage without noticing her. She turned away and walked across her ploughed field, trying to give the impression that she was examining the soil.

Later, as she was returning to her own house, she met Dick Moran coming out.

Dick was a handsome man in his middle forties, prosperous and well-dressed, a little fastidious in picking his way along the muddy path from the front door to his expensive car. He was always very affable, but behind the smiling face there was a sharp business brain. Biddy was always slightly wary of him, as indeed he was of her, because his friendship with Mary MacDermott lay like a rather dangerous rock beneath the smooth waters of their relationship, unmentioned but tacitly acknowledged.

Even as she now greeted Dick, Biddy could see in the background the lonely figure of her father moving in his slow, quiet fashion across the vegetable garden behind the house. A twinge of pity went through her. She had never been very close to him, but she knew that he hadn't done anything to deserve what was happening behind his back. She wondered if he had any suspicion of what was going on. She hoped for his own sake that he hadn't.

As usual, Dick Moran was smiling.

'Hi, Biddy.' He lowered his voice. 'You have visitors.'

'Visitors?'

'Your new neighbours. Mary's giving them tea.'

'Oh lord,' said Biddy. 'And will you just look at the cut of me!'

'Don't worry,' said Dick. 'They're the kind won't even notice. Not unless you're a sheep. See you again.'

There was nothing for it but to go inside and meet them. She removed her wellingtons in the small vestibule off the kitchen and replaced them with a pair of slippers. Then she glanced at her reflection in the wall-mirror and was appalled to see how untidy the wind had made her hair. There was no comb in the pocket of her anorak, so she had to use her fingers.

'Is that you, Biddy?' Her mother's voice came to her from the kitchen.

'Coming,' called Biddy.

When she entered the kitchen, the two men jumped to their feet.

'This is Biddy, my daughter,' said Mary. 'Biddy, these are the new neighbours. Dinny Byrne . . . and Miley.'

Miley stood back from her, nodding awkwardly, a shy smile on his face, his embarrassment matching her own, but Dinny, who had taken off his boots and was displaying a pair of heavy grey woollen socks with large holes in them, grabbed Biddy's hand and started to pump it up and down. He was a well-preserved man, still handsome, still conscious of his own masculinity and able to recognise a good-looking woman when he saw one. Evidently he had already made a favourable assessment of her mother.

'Are you codding me or what, Mary?' he asked. 'A young slip like yourself with a grown-up daughter! Will you go 'way!'

It was obvious that Dinny Byrne was a man who knew how to flatter a lady and there was an appreciative gleam in his eye as he looked at Biddy and continued to pump her hand.

Mary laughed. 'I've two grown-up daughters, if you want to know. The other one's in Dublin.'

'And this is the home-bird?' said Dinny.

'Biddy runs the place.'

Biddy retrieved her hand from Dinny's grasp. Her throat was tight with shyness.

'Sit down,' she said. 'Please.'

As the men resumed their seats, Dinny crossed one leg over the other, holding his dilapidated socks up as if for public display. Biddy could see that Miley was squirming with embarrassment, but Dinny was totally unabashed. He even seemed proud of the state of his socks and he wriggled his toes in case they had gone unnoticed.

'You know what you need, Dinny,' said Mary. 'You need a woman.'

'Begod, Mary, I'm open to offers.'

Miley did not join in the laughter. He spoke for the first time, deliberately changing the subject.

'He seems a very decent man.' They looked at him. ' Mr Moran. And a very *straight* man.'

'Yes,' said Biddy without conviction.

'But do you know what I'm going to tell you,' continued Miley. 'I've often been talking to Matt and he hardly ever mentions his father.'

'They don't get on,' said Biddy.

Mary said, 'Oh I wouldn't say that.'

'I would.' Biddy didn't see any reason why she should lie about it. 'His father leans on him.'

There was a rather awkward silence.

'Is there anything we can do to help you settle in?' asked Mary. 'On the farm, I mean.'

Dinny immediately launched into an exposition of his plans for sowing some early Queens in the hill field. He gave the impression of a man who had been tilling the soil for years, but Biddy could see from Miley's expression that he knew his father was merely putting on an act. He stood up nervously and walked over to the window, staring out while the old man rattled on.

'It's starting to look like rain,' said Miley suddenly. 'We'll have to get the furniture into the house.'

It cut short the agricultural homily. Despite Dinny's obvious reluctance to stir himself until he had drunk his cup of tea, Miley got him on his feet, made him put his boots back on and hurried him out the door, though not before they had accepted an invitation from Mary to come back later on for a proper meal.

When they had gone, Mary turned to her daughter.

'Well, what do you think?'

'Real mountainy men,' said Biddy, but she grinned to take the harm out of it. 'And the father's a right oul ram.'

Mary giggled. 'I know. But he's funny. What about the son?'

Biddy refused to be drawn. But she had to admit to herself that Miley Byrne seemed to be a decent, kindly sort of man, even if he knew very little about how to behave in company.

Over the next week she discovered that Miley knew even less about tillage farming than Dinny did and she found herself more and more slipping into the role of agricultural advisor to the father and son. When the contractor came to harrow the field for her early potatoes, she got him to do the hill field for the Byrnes as well, standing over him until he had finished the job to her satisfaction, accepting no excuses and allowing him take no short-cuts. She also showed the mountainy men how to recognise gangrene in the seed potatoes, what to sow and what to throw away.

Dinny objected at first to being corrected by what he called a 'young bit of a girl', but Miley was full of admiration for the way she had handled the contractor and for the general air of decisiveness about everything she did. As the days passed and the shyness between them diminished, Biddy found Miley very easy to talk to, though their conversations were almost totally confined to farming matters.

Then one evening he wandered by mistake into the children's disco she ran in the basement of Malone's pub in Glenroe. He had left his father drinking in the pub and had come down the stairs and into the darkened basement, under the impression that it was an adult disco. Unable to see properly in the gloom, he had joined awkwardly in the dancing.

When the set ended and the lights went up, he found himself surrounded by a crowd of young teenagers, who were highly amused to discover the large clumsy man in their midst. Miley was looking around him in wild alarm and thinking strongly of flight when he saw Biddy's familiar face. His relief was palpable.

Biddy had dressed herself up a bit that night and looked prettier than usual and, when they sat on the stairs together during one of the sets, she took advantage of his confusion to solicit his help with the children. He seemed willing enough to be dragged in, though she wished his acceptance had been couched in somewhat different terms.

What he said was, 'Sure, I might as well be in there with you as drinking above with me father.'

'Thanks very much,' said Biddy, unable to keep a touch of acerbity out of her voice.

Miley didn't appear to notice anything at all.

Lately Biddy had started to take more care of her appearance, even when she was merely working about the farm. She found herself glancing in the mirror more often before she went out and her shirts were changed more frequently and ironed more attentively. This hadn't gone unnoticed by her mother, who made a few sly remarks and smiled a few knowing smiles. Miley, however, seemed not to be aware of it, or if he was he gave no sign.

Sometimes she felt he didn't see her as a woman at all.

'Well, that's the way I want it,' she told herself. 'That's the way I've always wanted it.'

Then one day, quite unexpectedly, he invited her into the cottage and made her a cup of tea.

'Do you know what I'm going to tell you,' he said as he filled the two mugs, 'There's something definitely lacking in this house only I can't put my finger on it.'

Biddy looked around the bare room. Everything was lacking. It contained only the minimum of furniture and what there was was functional in the extreme. A real man's home, she thought, spare and cold and uninviting.

She said, 'It wouldn't take much to put it right.'

'I wouldn't mind spending a few pounds on it to make it a bit cosier. If I knew what to put in it.'

'There's an auction in Greystones next week,' said Biddy. 'I could go with you, if you like.'

'That would be nice,' said Miley.

There was a moment's silence. Miley seemed to be searching for words.

'Do you know who I haven't seen all week?' he said at last. 'Matt Moran.'

'He doesn't often come out this way.'

'What do you think of him?'

'He's very nice.'

'I thought that,' said Miley, grinning broadly at her.

'You thought what?'

'That you fancied him,' said Miley. 'I partly guessed that.'

'I don't fancy him,' Biddy snapped.

Miley was still smiling. 'He fancies you too.'

Biddy found herself really annoyed at the stupidity of the man. She glared at him.

'I do *not* fancy Matt Moran,' she said, emphasising the words, especially the negative.

Miley was suddenly deflated.

'I didn't mean to . . .' he began.

'I've more to be doing with my time than running after Matt Moran. Or any other man,' said Biddy.

'I know you have,' said Miley. 'Sure I know it well.'

'I don't want to hear any more about it,' said Biddy.

And no more was said on the subject. They finished their tea in silence. Biddy could feel her anger subsiding and she found herself wondering why the thought of 'fancying' Matt Moran should have so upset her. She glanced furtively at Miley, but he showed no outward emotion. She decided that all mountainy men were thick and unfeeling.

The trip to the auction in Greystones was very successful.

Biddy loved these occasions, the people crowded into the narrow, stuffy hall, the animated talk before the actual bidding began, then the droning voice of the auctioneer, the excitement as the bidding rose and the competition became more acute, and the final feeling of triumph when the desired article was knocked down to her. Miley, for his part, was content to sit back and leave it all in her hands, but she noticed, whenever she stole a glance at him, that he was taking everything in and knew exactly what was going on. He kept nodding approval as she bought four dining chairs, a table, a sideboard, two easy chairs and a couple of other odds and ends.

When the auction had finished they had to push their way out through the chattering crowd into the street.

'How much did we spend?' asked Miley.

Biddy did a quick calculation.

'Hundred and eighty. And there'll be commission on that. It'll be nearer one-ninety before you're finished.'

Miley was pleased.

'That's grand. You could go mad in there very easy.'

'Yeah,' said Biddy. 'A pity we missed the standing clock.'

'Sure haven't we got a clock on the cooker.'

She laughed at him, but hadn't the heart to tell him why.

'Anyway, we did well getting the two easy chairs,' said Miley.

They walked down the street together in a companionable silence, but when he asked her to go into a cafe and have a sandwich she refused. She didn't want to say no, but was unable to help herself.

'I have to get back home,' she said, conjuring up a picture of mammoth, urgent tasks awaiting her attention.

Miley didn't argue. Instead he asked her if he could borrow her drill plough for his cabbages. Biddy agreed — on condition that he help her in the children's disco on Saturday night.

'You're a right chancer,' said Miley.

Biddy grinned. 'It won't kill you.'

Suddenly she was seized around the waist in a rough grasp and squeezed hard. It was Paddy Maher. His vegetable van was parked further up the road, where his sister Nuala was dealing with the customers.

'Are you having a day off?' asked Paddy. 'You should've told me and I'd've made meself available.' He looked at Miley. 'Is this the new boy-friend?'

'The new neighbour.'

Biddy introduced them.

'I met your oul fella,' said Paddy. He was a stocky man in his thirties, who had an air of aggressive mockery about him. Biddy knew it was more of a front than a reality, but at the same time she was also aware of Paddy's instinctive aversion to what he called 'blow-ins'. She could see that Miley didn't quite know how to answer Paddy's mocking grin.

'I hear you're growing a few spuds,' said Paddy.

'And a bit of cabbage,' said Miley.

'Maybe I can take some stuff off your hands.'

'Maybe you can.'

'There's a lot of pitfalls in this business.'said Paddy, with his little half-smile. 'A lot to learn.'

Miley said, 'Biddy here'll keep an eye on me.'

'She'd want to,' said Paddy.

Biddy hated Paddy for being so rude to a newcomer to the town, though Miley appeared not to take offence. In fact, he merely seemed baffled by Paddy's attitude and incapable of dealing with it.

He asked Biddy if she wanted a lift back to Glenroe and, when she made her usual negative response, he took his leave of them and drove away in his battered car.

Biddy immediately turned on Paddy and waded into him for his rudeness. He was genuinely surprised by her attack.

'I wasn't rude,' said Paddy. 'Anyway, if you like him so much, why didn't you take the lift home in his car?'

Biddy had no answer to that. It was always the same with her, an instant negative reaction to any offer, especially from a man, something which she appeared to have no control over and which she invariably regretted later on. She scowled at Paddy and went stamping off to find her mother's car.

'What's wrong with you?' Mary asked her as they drove home.

'What'd be wrong with me,' Biddy snapped at her. 'I did everything I came into Greystones to do. I got all the furniture at a decent price. I don't know why you have to be thinking that there's something wrong with me!'

'Excuse me,' said Mary.

There was no further conversation for the rest of the journey.

Next Saturday night Miley did turn up for the children's disco as he had promised. He had a big story for her concerning Dinny's hens. Apparently his father had met somebody in the pub the evening before and had done a deal while he was in his cups. Next morning Miley had awakened to the sound of a rooster and discovered a dozen hens scrabbling around outside the cottage door.

Biddy found herself laughing, but Miley couldn't see the funny side of it.

'We have to watch the money, Biddy,' he said.

'There'll be nothing coming in for months and we've a tractor to buy. What's left in the bank won't last forever.'

'What is it only a few hens,' said Biddy.

'He's in the pub every night till closing. It won't last long that way.'

'Maybe you'll be able to sell the eggs.'

'And maybe pigs'll fly.'

When the disco had ended and the last of the children had gone home, Miley asked her to come into the pub for a drink.

'Ah no thanks, Miley. I'm tired.' She hated herself even as she said the words. 'I think I'll go home.'

'Whatever you say.'

Biddy didn't move.

'Maybe just the one,' said Miley, 'and then I'll run you home.'

'I don't want to drag you away.'

'Divil the drag. The one pint'll do me.'

'I hate the way they all look at you in there,' said Biddy. 'And pass remarks.'

'I know,' said Miley. 'I hate it myself.'

As they stood there, the door of the pub opened and a group of young men emerged. They all greeted Biddy by name. One of them was Matt Moran, a little flushed from drink. He came across to them.

'Are you coming or going?' he asked.

'We were just discussing that,' said Miley.

'Well, I tell you what,' said Matt. 'There's a dance in Wicklow and a choice of two hooleys after it. Will you come?'

Miley said, 'Sure, we weren't asked.'

'I'm asking you,' said Matt. 'Come on, Biddy. You know all the crowd.'

'Yes, but I can't,' said Biddy.

'Why can't you?'

'Because Miley just asked me to come for a drink.'

Matt looked from one to the other and smiled.

'Fair enough. Be good now.'

And he was gone. Miley looked a bit baffled.

Biddy said, 'You didn't want to go, did you?'

'Oh no, no.'

'Well, come on, then.'

Biddy led the way into the pub. It was quite crowded inside. Paddy Maher and his sister sat in a corner. At the bar were Stephen Brennan and some of his friends. Miley had met Stephen a few nights before and he now had to acknowledge the broad smile that was beamed in their direction. Other heads turned to survey the new arrivals. There were little nudges and whispers.

Biddy found an empty table as far as possible from the bar. They both sat, embarrassed, glancing furtively around. Miley made several ineffectual attempts to catch the eye of the waiter.

Stephen Brennan called across, 'Where's the boss, Miley?'

'I left him at home,' said Miley.

Stephen's grin grew wider.

'You were just right. Sure, he'd only be in the way, wha'!'

There were chuckles from some of the others. Biddy could feel her face growing redder. She grabbed the passing waiter by the arm.

'Jimmy, bring us a bottle of lager and a pint of stout.'

There was a pause. Then Miley said, 'I hope I wasn't in the way there.'

'When?'

'When Matt was saying about the dance. I thought maybe I was in the way.'

'Why?' There was a growing impatience in Biddy's voice.

'I'd say you wanted to go.'

'I didn't.'

'I'd say you did.'

'Look,' said Biddy, as if explaining to a child, 'if I'd wanted to go I'd have gone.'

'Well maybe you would have,' persisted Miley, 'only for I was in the way.'

Biddy's exasperation burst out.

'Will you stop saying that!'

It wasn't the most successful of nights. Conversation between them was very desultory. Miley continued to look apologetic for being alive and in the wrong place at the wrong time; Biddy became more irritated and consequently more withdrawn and silent as the time wore on. Every time she raised her head she found someone or other grinning knowingly in her direction.

Eventually she could stand it no longer.

'I'd like to go home now, Miley,' she said.

Immediately he was on his feet, full of concern and attention. As they left the pub there were some more nudges and sly remarks, which Biddy ignored as best she could, but she knew that her cheeks were blazing. She led the way out to the car park without a word and slumped down into the seat, her hands plunged deep into the pockets of her anorak.

When they reached the MacDermott house they both got out of the car and stood awkwardly outside the front door. There was silence between them.

'Well . . .' said Biddy. 'Time I was going in.'

'Aye,' said Miley. Then, with a great effort, 'What are you doing next week?'

'We'll be starting the barley on Monday . . .' Biddy began.

'No, I mean next weekend,' said Miley. 'It's Easter.'

'Yeah, I know.' She waited for him to continue.

Miley said, 'There's a dance in the Royal. And a candle-light supper.'

'I know,' said Biddy.

'Well, would you like to go?'

'With you?'

'Yeah. That's if you want to.'

'Yeah, all right,' said Biddy. 'But you don't have to ask me.'

'I know that,' said Miley, 'but I want you to come anyway.'

'Do you?' asked Biddy.

'Sure, after all the help you've given me, it's the least I could do.'

It wasn't the most perfect of reasons for asking her out.

'Goodnight.'

Biddy left him abruptly and went inside.

During the following week she was very busy. The big event was the meeting of the Growers' Association, which was held in the basement of Malone's pub, where Biddy held the children's disco.

The meeting was a noisy one. For some time there had been general dissatisfaction with the price they had been getting in the Dublin Market and the growers present said so strongly and loudly, especially Paddy Maher. Dick Moran, who was responsible for transporting the vegetables to the market and selling them, had his own explanation for the situation, an explanation which naturally absolved himself from any possible blame and shifted the responsibility onto the lack of a governmental policy on marketing.

Biddy found herself becoming more and more angry at what she recognised as a manipulation of the meeting and soon she was on her feet to argue for the need for self-help. As usual she had to speak through a barrage of 'Oh here she goes again!' and 'We're off now!', but she stuck to her guns and had her say, even if in the end she found herself out-manoeuvred by the wily auctioneer and voted down.

All the while she was conscious of Miley staring wide-eyed at her from the back of the room.

The next day she went into Dublin and bought a new frock, telling herself that she was doing it for Easter. She also paid a visit to the hairdresser and had herself a perm. She even contemplated a new pair of shoes, but eventually decided against the extravagance.

Her mother watched all these preparations with some amusement. She decided against saying anything to Biddy herself, but when her younger daughter, Carol, came home from her Dublin bank for the Easter holidays, they had a quiet laugh together about it.

'This Miley Byrne must be a remarkable fellow if he can make Biddy get herself a perm,' said Carol.

A year younger than Biddy and a great deal prettier, Carol was wise in the ways of the world, at least as far as the Leeson Street strip and its immediate environs were concerned. She was never without a boyfriend and very rarely with the same one longer than a couple of weeks.

On the night of the dance Carol and Mary watched Biddy titivating herself in front of the mirror in the sitting-room.

'A remarkable man,' said Carol.

'Don't be silly,' said Biddy. 'How do I look?'

'Smashing,' said Carol. 'You'll have him foaming at the mouth with passion.'

Mary said, 'Very nice. I like your hair that way.'

'I was thinking of doing something else with it,' said Biddy.

'Like what?'

'A bit of deep pink.'

'Fabulous,' said Carol.

'Biddy, you wouldn't.' Mary sounded genuinely alarmed.

'Why not?' said Biddy. 'It'd make a change.'

'You'd frighten the life out of poor Miley,' said Mary.

'He must be easily frightened,' said Carol.

Biddy laughed. 'It'd be nearly worth it, just to see his face.'

Carol said, 'Do you like him?'

Biddy was very non-committal. 'Ah, he's all right.'

'I think she does, Carol,' said Mary.

'Mam, will you stop!'

'Stop what?'

'He's ten years older than I am,' said Biddy, trying to put conviction into her voice. 'He's not very bright, he's not very rich and he's not very handsome.'

'Yes, but he's nice,' said Mary. 'And I'll tell you, Carol, he'll be here ready and willing on the stroke of nine.'

'That doesn't mean anything,' said Biddy.

'Take it from me,' said Mary, 'it means quite a lot.'

At that moment the front doorbell rang.

'What'd I tell you?' laughed Mary. 'Right on the dot.'

'Oh lord,' said Biddy. 'Stall him off for a minute, somebody.'

'I'll go,' said Carol.

Carol went to open the hall-door. Biddy gathered her things together, had a final quick look in the mirror, did a twirl for Mary's approval and went out to greet her date.

She found him in the hall dressed in a tuxedo, but without the bow-tie, which he had failed to manage and had put in his pocket. He was clutching a box of chocolates.

He was also staring at Carol as if he had never seen anything like her before in his life.

'I see you've met Carol,' said Biddy, trying to ignore the sinking feeling in her stomach.

'What?' said Miley abstractedly.

Carol smiled. 'We introduced ourselves.'

'Well, come on,' said Biddy, going out the hall door.

'Have a good time,' said Carol.

'Thanks,' said Miley. 'Thanks very much.'

'Come on, Miley,' said Biddy more loudly.

She understood only too well the expression on Miley's face and the glazed look in his eyes.

## · CHAPTER TWO ·

# THE MACDERMOTT STORY

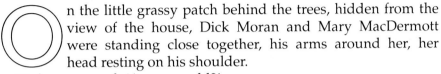n the little grassy patch behind the trees, hidden from the view of the house, Dick Moran and Mary MacDermott were standing close together, his arms around her, her head resting on his shoulder.

Dick murmured, 'Are you cold?'

She snuggled closer.

'I feel fine.'

'I suppose there's a good fire inside in the house?'

'Should be.'

'Going to waste.'

Mary stirred in his arms.

'Now don't say that, Dick. You know we can't.'

'I don't see why not,' said Dick. 'It isn't as if I've never been in your house before.'

'Yes. But those times were . . . official.'

'We're not exactly the age for coortin' behind bushes.'

'Oh I don't know.' Mary smiled in the darkness. 'Doesn't it take you back?'

'I'm not sure that I want to go back,' said Dick, tightening his arms around her.

He bent his head and kissed her. Then he asked the question he asked her every time they were together.

'Can't we get away somewhere?'

'Where?'

'It wouldn't matter. Anywhere. Some place we could relax. No hiding.'

Mary said, 'I could make it to Dublin . . . maybe one day next week.'

'As long as I got you home in time for tea.'

She reacted to the tone of his voice.

'You know how it is, Dick!'

'Yes, I know.' He paused. 'But it wasn't a day-trip I was thinking of.'

She looked up at him.

'Couldn't we manage a weekend?' he asked.

'I wish we could, but . . .'

17

'But what?'

'What would I say?'

He shrugged.

'Bridge. Don't you have weekend Bridge Congresses?'

'I only go to the local ones.'

'But there must be others. Further away. Where you'd have to stay over.'

'Yes, but I couldn't . . .'

He released her suddenly.

'All right. It was just a suggestion.'

'Don't be annoyed, dear,' she pleaded with him. 'It's as bad for me as it is for you.'

'Is it?'

'You know it is!'

'Let's go into the house,' Dick said. 'We'll turn on all the lights and leave all the doors open and speak in loud voices. What's wrong with that?'

Mary shook her head.

He was angry now.

'All right!'

He turned away from her and walked down the driveway. She followed him.

'No, Dick. Come back.'

When they saw Dinny on the darkened driveway he was apparently in the act of rising from his knees.

He smiled at Dick and Mary and held up something like a piece of string.

'The oul' lace is after breaking on me,' he said.

Dick said coldly, 'Goodnight, Dinny.'

'Goodnight to you, Dick. And to you, Mary.'

Dick walked quickly past him to where his car was parked. Mary hesitated a moment and then went after Dick. He was already in the car and fumbling with the ignition key.

Mary spoke though the open window, 'Dick, don't go . . .'

The engine roared into life. Dick stared ahead of him stonily.

'Do you think he heard?' asked Mary anxiously.

'It wouldn't be for want of trying.'

'I'm sorry, Dick.'

'It's all right.'

There was a cold edge to Dick's voice.

'I'll ring you tomorrow,' said Mary.

Dick nodded and drove away.

Mary watched the tail-lights disappearing down the driveway. Then she turned and walked back towards the house. Dinny was still standing where they had left him.

'That's a hardy one,' he said.

'Yes.'

She found it impossible to say anything else.

'Would you have the kettle on?' asked Dinny.

Mary didn't look at him.

'Not tonight, Dinny,' she said.

She walked away from him without a backward glance, but she knew that he was still standing there, looking after her.

It was always the same, she thought. Somebody was always looking at her. Looking at *them*. Nobody ever said anything, but the looks were enough. Of course she knew, they *both* knew, that in a small town like Glenroe it was asking too much to expect that anything could be kept from the neighbours. Especially . . . She shied away from the word. She had got into the habit of shying away from unpleasant things.

Later, as she lay in bed listening to Michael's shallow breathing, she wondered how much Dinny had heard. He must have heard something.

She tried to recall what they had been saying before they knew he was there. They hadn't attempted to keep their voices down. Dick had been too annoyed for that, too disappointed to bother about who might be listening.

It was all right for him, she thought with a tinge of bitterness. His wife had walked out on him ten years ago, without even saying goodbye, without making any attempt to get in touch with him until that one phone call two years later, asking him to allow her to come back home. That was just like Ruth, making her own decisions without considering the hurt they inflicted, and then expecting to be welcomed back as if nothing had happened. Dick had refused, of course, saying that the children had got used to being without their mother and that there was no point trying to patch the broken pieces of their marriage together.

Yes, it was all right for Dick, thought Mary. He was tough. But not for her. She hadn't even his relative freedom, his . . . well, justification. Her husband was lying here beside her, his very presence a condemnation of her actions over the past few years.

If only things had been different twenty-five years ago. If only she hadn't been so young and so vulnerable when her father had died, so alone and so lost, with no mother to advise her. If only she hadn't married then, if she had had the strength to wait, she might later on have been able to welcome the attraction she felt towards Dick Moran, have been able to enter into this relationship with him with no recriminations, none of this dreadful guilt.

But she hadn't waited. She had married. No, not really married — she had merely substituted one father for another.

Michael MacDermott and John Leavy had been close friends, the middle aged bachelor farming the land beside the middle-aged widower, two taciturn men walking the fields together, talking about their problems, drinking their companionable pints in the pub at the end of the day, sharing their thoughts as much as two such naturally reserved men were capable of doing.

When John Leavy died suddenly in the winter of 1957, Michael was as grief-stricken as John's young daughter. He comforted the seventeen-year-old girl in his own quiet way, arranged the funeral and the rest of the unpleasant residuals of death with a mute delicacy which touched Mary's heart. He took to calling around to the house and sitting there for long hours, watching her as she went about her daily tasks, emanating a silent sympathy and affection much more powerful than words, filling the empty space in her life with his consoling and strengthening presence.

And when finally, a year later, he asked her to marry him, she found it impossible to say no.

Of course, Ruth Sheridan had advised her against it. But then, it was easier for Ruth. It was always easier for other people, Mary thought with a sigh.

Ruth had everything. She was at university, mixing with the fast-moving set up in Dublin, while Mary remained at home on the farm, looking after her father. Ruth had no such responsibilities to tie her down and prevent her from living her life to the full.

And Ruth had the young Dick Moran totally enraptured by her dark eyes and her knowledgeable ways. Not that Mary envied her Dick's undoubted devotion. Not at first. That would come later.

'You're mad,' Ruth said. 'He's too old for you. He's almost as old as your father, for God's sake.'

'He's kind, Ruth.'

'Kind, be damned! That's no basis for a marriage. Think about it, Mary. When you're forty he'll be in his seventies. What'll you do then?'

'But there are other considerations,' Mary said. 'Security. Stability.'

Ruth exploded. 'Who wants security!'

But security was precisely what Mary wanted. Without her father she felt totally forsaken and unable to cope.

'It's all right for you, Ruth . . .'

And so she had married Michael.

And it hadn't been too bad initially. He *was* kind and considerate and undemanding. And then the children came, two beautiful little girls to mother and shower her affections on. In those early years she felt herself truly blessed and fulfilled. The two farms were joined together to form a sizeable holding. There was plenty of money to help her forget the lack of a consuming romantic passion in her life. She told herself that she didn't need all the sexual thrills that Ruth seemed to set so much store by. She had her home and her children and didn't ask for anything more.

In time, and inevitably, Ruth found herself pregnant. Life in the fast-lane, Mary thought rather smugly, wasn't all a bed of roses. When Ruth came to cry on her shoulder and complain about the tyranny of nature, Mary offered her what comfort she could, but she couldn't help feeling a complacent satisfaction that she had managed to avoid the unpleasant situation Ruth had brought upon herself.

Ruth married the handsome Dick Moran, the father of her unborn son, and settled down, somewhat reluctantly, into the domesticity her position demanded.

Perhaps 'settled down' was not quite the appropriate phrase.

From the standpoint of her own ordered existence, Mary watched the Morans make rather heavy weather of their marriage. Ruth was still the wilful and volatile creature she had been before she became a wife and mother; Dick was still the handsome man who continued to attract and welcome the attentions of other women. From an early stage cracks began to appear in the facade of their marriage. More and more frequently, Mary found herself the recipient of tearful confidences from the reluctant mother. Even with her two sons, Paul and Matt, to take care of, Ruth seemed both unable and unwilling to resign herself to her new life.

And then, after twelve years of uneasy coexistence with her husband and family, and with something of the same inevitability which had characterised her entry into marriage, Ruth one day packed her bags and disappeared from Glenroe.

Dick was devastated by her unexpected departure, hurt and betrayed as a husband and father, outraged that any woman should have decided to leave *him*. And, as his wife before him had done, he sought sympathy from Mary.

\*    \*    \*    \*    \*

Mary sighed again. It had seemed so innocent at the start, just one friend consoling another. But it hadn't remained so for long. With her own silent husband growing old beside her, it had been all too easy to allow her sympathy for Dick Moran to blossom into something more vital and dangerous.

For the first time she had found how compelling it was to love a man and how simple it was to cross the tenuous dividing-line between friendship and romantic attachment. It hadn't seemed very wrong at first and then it had become so all-consuming that it was unthinkable to imagine it as anything but right and proper.

No, that wasn't true. It wasn't right and proper. And whenever Dick and herself were seen together in questionable circumstances, it became the rather sordid affaire it really was.

And now Dinny Byrne, her new neighbour, had joined the people who knew.

It was all too disturbing. She tried to put it out of her mind and go to sleep. Beside her, Michael turned over with a little groan. An old man now, as old as her father would have been, he had grown ever more silent as the years had gone by. No wonder that Dinny Byrne, when he had seen Michael for the first time, had imagined him to be an old labouring man working on the farm.

She remembered what Dinny had said that day.

'Is he able to do much?'

'Who?'

'The oul fella.'

'Oh yes.'

She had rather enjoyed the mistake at the time.

'He looks fit enough for his age, all right,' Dinny had said. 'How long have you had him?'

'Oh a long time. Twenty-five years.'

Dinny had plunged ahead in his ignorance.

'Begod, you're very lucky. It's hard to find good labouring men these days.'

She had said deliberately, with a wry little smile, 'He's not a labouring man, Dinny. He's the boss. He's my husband.'

She could still see the surprise on Dinny's face. For once he had been left with nothing to say for himself.

And now her children were reared, Carol away working in a bank in Dublin and Biddy minding the farm, doing most of the work her father was no longer able to do. Both of them were already older than she had been when she married. Well, at least they hadn't made the same mistake as their mother.

'Think of it, Mary! When you're forty, he'll be in his seventies!'

She finally fell asleep with Ruth's words running around in her brain.

For the next couple of days she kept herself busy around the house and managed to avoid meeting Dinny face to face. Biddy always said of her mother that she flew through her housework in order to be able to dress herself up and get out and about to play her bridge and golf. Mary didn't accept that this was altogether true. She kept a good house for other reasons as well: a sense of duty towards Michael — not that he appeared to notice the results of her work — and in order to assuage the guilt which beset her every now and again when she allowed herself to think of it.

She was almost glad when, a couple of days later, she heard the news that Miley's trailer had been wrecked during the night. It would give them all something to occupy their minds. She hoped that Dinny especially would be so distracted that he would forget what he had seen. Seen? Surely he hadn't . . . ! But there *had* been a kiss. At least one. A lot. Her face reddened at the thought and she worked harder than ever in an effort to drive it away.

The morning after the wrecking of the trailer the postman arrived with a parcel addressed to Mr Miles Byrne. He asked Mary to take it, to save him the added journey across to the cottage. She looked through the window at where the father and son were surveying the damaged vehicle. Biddy had gone up to the back field, Michael was in the cowshed, so there was no way out of it. She would have to go and deliver the parcel herself.

Well, it might as well be now as later. She braced herself and went out.

'A parcel for you, Miley,' she said as brightly as she could. 'Morning, Dinny.'

Miley took the parcel.

'It's me jingle,' he said.

'Your what?'

'Me diddli-eye-do,' said Miley. 'It's either Dr Zhivago, or the Blue Danube.'

'Is that what you picked?' said Mary, glad to have a safe subject to talk about.

'I like the classical,' said Miley. 'But, sure,what's the use of a jingle when I've no trailer to do me vegetable round with.'

He walked sadly away with his parcel.

Now she and Dinny were alone together. Mary waited for some comment.

'Wouldn't he put years on you?' said Dinny. 'Moaning all over the place. The hens is better company. And I'm tired telling him it's only a trailer.'

A thought struck her.

'Look, Dinny, we've got an old trailer lying in the barn. Miley is very welcome to it.'

'Begod, that's very decent of you, Mary.'

'Oh it's nothing,' said Mary.

'It's plenty.' said Dinny emphatically. 'I'll go and tell him right away.'

'Before you go, Dinny . . .'

Dinny paused.

'Ay?'

Mary swallowed, then plunged in.

'About the other night . . .'

'What other night was that?'

She couldn't be sure whether his look was innocent or deceiving. But having started, she had to go on.

'You met me in the drive. With Dick Moran.'

'Oh ay, ay.'

Was he secretly laughing at her?

She said, blushing slightly, 'I'd just as soon you didn't mention it to anyone.'

'Sure, why would I do that?' asked Dinny disarmingly.

'Well, it might just come out in talk — you know the way.'

Dinny laughed.

'Arragh not at all, Mary. I wouldn't have remembered it only you brought it up.'

She immediately regretted having raised the subject at all. But it was done now.

She put on her warmest smile.

'Would you like a cup of tea?'

'Begod, Mary, I thought you'd never ask. Wait till I tell the young lad about the trailer and I'll be over in two ticks.'

As he walked away, his smile was as bright as her own. She turned quickly back to the house, to hide her burning cheeks.

But when Dinny came in later on for his cup of tea, he made no reference to their earlier conversation and nothing in his manner indicated that he even remembered it.

Mary began to breathe more easily.

The next day she went into Glenroe to do some shopping and she bumped into Dick Moran in the Main Street. He seemed to have regained his customary good humour and greeted her with a smile. They stood chatting, as any friends might who had stopped to pass the time of day, and they were careful to wave hello to passers-by as if they were doing no more than talking about the weather.

'Any word from our friend with the broken laces?' asked Dick.

'No,' said Mary.

'So he heard nothing?'

'Apparently not.'

There was a pause and then Mary said deliberately, 'Ballybunnion.'

'I beg your pardon?'

'There is a Bridge Congress in Ballybunnion next weekend,' said Mary. 'I'm thinking of going.'

'I see,' said Dick. 'Where do I book for?'

'I'll leave that to you.'

'Wherever you like.'

'You don't have to sound so enthusiastic,' said Dick.

'I'm going, amn't I?' said Mary, still smiling though there was a hint of anger in her voice. 'I don't have to play a trumpet as well, do I?'

'If you don't want to go. . . .'

'I wouldn't be going if I didn't want to!'

'All right, all right,' said Dick, waving at Stephen Brennan on the opposite side of the street.

'I'm sorry,' said Mary. 'I've been a bit upset lately.'

'I know a cure for the upsets,' said Dick. 'If you drive into Bray on Saturday afternoon I'll meet you there. Two o'clock at the Town Hall. OK?'

So simple, she thought as she drove home. All the big decisions are made simply. No doubt some day when the atomic button is pressed it will be done almost as an afterthought by some bemused politician with too much on his mind to realise the importance of his action.

When she was having a cup of tea with Biddy and Dinny that evening she was careful to toss the remark across the table as if it had just occurred to her.

'By the way, Biddy,' she said, 'have you anything planned for next weekend?'

'No,' said Biddy. 'Why?'

'I might be away on Saturday night.'

'Where?'

'Ballybunnion,' said Mary, pouring tea. 'I'm playing bridge.' She passed Dinny his cup and smiled at him. He looked back at her with no expression at all on his face.

Mary told herself that she had carried it off very well. She drank her tea and chatted gaily and ignored the faint tremors of misgiving which niggled at her.

Michael made no comment when she told him she would be away. But then he seldom made any comment about anything.

On the Saturday afternoon she packed her bag and drove into Bray to keep her rendezvous with Dick Moran. She went secure in the knowledge that she had made all the domestic arrangements necessary to look after the needs of her husband and daughter while she was away. It was a comforting feeling.

But the weekend in Cork wasn't a success.

Oh, the hotel was very swish and Dick was all love and attention. He bought her flowers and chocolates. They had dinner by candlelight. They danced in the hotel ballroom to a band which played all the appropriate romantic tunes from her teenage years and made her eyes glisten with tears for her lost youth. Their room was very comfortable. Dick couldn't have been more gentle and understanding.

She should have been very happy. But still . . .

When they were having breakfast in bed on the Sunday morning, Dick said suddenly, 'You're not enjoying yourself, Mary.'

'Oh I am,' she protested. 'It's just . . .'

'You feel bad,' said Dick.

'Yes. A little.'

'You feel good and you feel bad.'

'I can't help that,' said Mary. 'You don't have to make fun of it.'

But Dick was very serious.

'It's no fun, Mary. It hasn't been fun for a while now.'

She had nothing to say.

'Maybe you want to call it off.'

She said quickly, 'I didn't say that.' Then she added, 'They all know.'

'Of course they know,' said Dick. 'They're not fools.'

'Yes,' said Mary. 'I suppose I never really thought of it before.'

Dick said, 'I think I'm right. You *do* want to call it off. Maybe we should take things easy for a while. Not see so much of each other.'

She nodded.

'Not around Glenroe anyway,' said Dick. 'But we could manage another weekend.'

'No.'

'Somewhere else next time?'

'No, Dick. This is the last time.'

They drove back to Glenroe in a mood very different from that in which they had set out.

No, it hadn't been a success.

At home she found Michael even more silent than ever, if that were possible. She tried to tell him about the hands she had supposedly played, how she had lost and won by turns, but he showed very little interest and in the end she gave it up as a bad job. Even Biddy paid scant attention to the gossip Mary invented, but then Biddy was having her own troubles with Miley and couldn't be expected to be vitally concerned about the niceties of a game she herself didn't play, or the idle chatter of those who did.

Mary knew that she should have been happy that the weekend was safely over and that she hadn't been found out. But she wasn't. She felt irritable and moody and went about snapping at everyone.

Her anger came to a boil when she had tea with Dinny in the sitting room the next evening. Since his arrival in Glenroe he had become a frequent visitor to the MacDermott house. Although he never came unless invited, he always managed to manipulate either Mary or Biddy into asking him, with the result that he drank innumerable cups of tea and stayed long hours chatting with Michael. Or, to be more truthful, chatting *to* Michael. These sessions invariably consisted of a monologue from Dinny punctuated by the very odd comment from Michael.

This evening Michael had gone to bed early and Mary had decided to bring Dinny's tea into the sitting room, because Carol was home and was filling the kitchen with noise and steam from the washing-machine.

When Mary entered the room with the tray, she found Dinny examining a silver cup and some glassware which were on the sideboard. He turned as she came in.

'I was just looking at your cut glass and things.'

'They're prizes,' said Mary, not without a little pride.

She set the tray down on an occasional table.

'I thought that,' said Dinny. 'From the Bridge?'

'Yes. Mostly.'

'I thought that,' said Dinny.

He took his cup and stirred the tea thoughtfully.

He asked, 'Did you win anything at the weekend?'

Mary looked quickly at him, but Dinny was concentrating on his tea. 'No.'

'I suppose you can't win all the time,' he said. 'Did you not play well?

'Not very,' said Mary.

She handed him a scone. He bit into it ruminatively before he spoke again.

'Of course, you have to have a partner for Bridge,' he said. 'Maybe it was your partner didn't play well?'

27

'One or the other. What does it matter!'

Mary didn't want to pursue the topic.

'Divil the matter,' said Dinny. 'All the same in a thousand years.'

After a pause, he added, 'Twasn't Molly, was it? Your partner, I mean.'

Mary put down her cup sharply. She could feel resentment rising inside her.

'Weren't you in the pub at the weekend?'

'I was.'

'And didn't you see Molly there?'

Dinny affected a sudden return of memory.

'Oh begod, that's right. So she . . .'

'So you knew it wasn't Molly,' Mary interrupted him tartly.

Dinny started to mumble a disclaimer, but Mary wasn't prepared to let him away with it.

'In fact, you knew very well who my partner was. You heard us talking about it.'

'I don't follow you at all, Mary.'

'That night in the drive. With Dick Moran. You heard everything.'

Dinny protested, 'Indeed I did not! Wasn't I only passing by . . .'

'You heard everything we said.'

Dinny chewed on his scone, his head bent.

'Sure, he doesn't even play the game. He told me that,' he said at length.

'That's right, ' said Mary. 'He doesn't. And I wasn't playing either . . . not last weekend.'

She waited for him to speak, but he said nothing.

'That seems to have silenced you, Dinny. You usually have plenty to say.'

He spoke then, very quietly.

'Tisn't my business.'

'And when did that ever stop you?'

Dinny finished his cup of tea. He stood up and moved towards the door.

'I'll say nothing.'

'No,' flared Mary. 'You'll say it all later. To you  friends in the pub.'

Dinny paused at the door. He spoke very mildly.

'No. I don't talk about you, Mary. There's enough doing that.'

She said bitterly, 'You mean you're worried about my reputation?'

'Why wouldn't I be,' he said. 'You've been very good to Miley and me. And we're fond of you.'

Mary bit off the sharp retort which was on the tip of her tongue.

'You'd better go now.'

He nodded and turned to the door again. As he left the room, Biddy came in. She greeted them both, but Dinny walked out without another word. Biddy was surprised.

'What's wrong with him?'

Mary was silent. Biddy tried again.

'Mam . . .'

Mary snapped, 'Oh don't keep on, Biddy!'

'Sorry,' said Biddy. She waited for Mary to speak again.

Eventually, Mary said, 'Apparently he worries about me.'

'What's wrong with that?'

'Who asked him to?' said Mary. Then she added, 'He said people were talking about me.'

'So they are,' said Biddy very quietly.

They stared at one another for a long moment.

'You have to expect it, Mam. People aren't blind. Sure, everybody knows it. Why do you pretend they don't?'

It took Mary a few moments to find her voice again.

'Are you shocked?'

Biddy shook her head.

'At first I was. Then I got used to it, used to wonder what kind of an evening you had when you went out. I wanted to ask you. But I didn't, because I knew you didn't want me to.'

She sat down on the settee beside Mary.

'How *was* the weekend?'

Mary smiled ruefully.

'It wasn't a great success.'

'I'll wet another pot of tea,' said Biddy. 'For the two of us.'

Later, when the two girls had gone out, Biddy to the cinema with Miley, and Carol on some expedition of her own, Mary sat alone in the kitchen. The scene with Dinny had upset her more than she had realised at the time, because then she had been sustained by her anger. Now she felt really drained and depressed. And to add to her gloom was the fact that Biddy knew about herself and Dick.

Oh, her daughter had been very kind and understanding, but that she knew at all filled Mary with a deep sense of shame. It was all wrong. And it would have to end.

Having made up her mind, and before she could have second thoughts about it, she stood up and went to the phone.

Dick answered almost immediately.

'Mary?' he said with obvious pleasure. 'You're not going to believe this, but I was just sitting here thinking about you and . . .'

She cut him short.

'Listen to me, Dick. I've got something to say to you. Something very important.'

'What's wrong?'

His pleasure had vanished. Now there was only anxiety in his voice.

'There's nothing wrong,' said Mary. 'No, that's not true. Every-thing's wrong. Everybody knows about us. And . . .' He interrupted her in his turn.

'Are you alone?

'Yes, of course I'm alone. But that has nothing to . . .'

'Where's Michael?'

'He's in bed. We're going to have to end it, Dick. I just can't go on living like this . . .'

'I'm coming over,' said Dick.

'No, Dick. You can't!'

'I'll be there in fifteen minutes.'

'Dick!'

But he had already put down the phone.

Mary waited in a fever of anxiety. She couldn't sit still. She walked from the kitchen to the foot of the stairs, listened a moment, went into the sitting room, sat down, stood up, returned to the hall and listened again. There was no sound. She quietly mounted the stairs to the bed-room. The door was ajar. Michael was sleeping soundly, his breathing slow and regular. Very carefully Mary drew the door closed. Then she descended the stairs again on tiptoe.

When she heard the sound of the car coming up the driveway, she went to the hall-door and opened it. Dick pulled up in his usual place some distance away from the house. She heard the car door close gently and the crunch of his approaching footsteps. When he approached the hall-door, she went a few steps to meet him.

'Dick, this is madness!'

He put his arms around her and kissed her.

'Inside.'

'No. Please . . .'

'Don't worry. I'll be quiet.'

With a firm arm around her, he guided her into the hall and shut the door quietly behind them.

'Kitchen or sitting room?'

'All right. The sitting room.'

They went into the sitting room. Dick very carefully closed the door.

'Now,' he said. 'What's all this about?'

'We're going to have to stop seeing each other,' said Mary. She was trying desperately to recapture the resolution she had felt before he had kissed her and overwhelmed her with his presence.

'What's happened?'

'Biddy knows.'

'Biddy? Is that all?' The relief in his voice was clear.

'Isn't that enough?'

He held out his hands to her and she went to his arms.

'I thought you were going to tell me that Michael knew.'

'Oh God, no!'

'Listen, Mary,' said Dick. 'Biddy has known about us for a long time.'

'I didn't know she knew,' Mary wailed.

'You did. Only you wouldn't admit it to yourself,' said Dick. 'So nothing has changed.'

'You don't understand, Dick. My own daughter!'

His arms tightened around her and she could feel the last of her resolve slipping away. His voice seemed to come to her from a distance.

'Nothing has changed, Mary. Nothing. And we're going on as we always have done.'

She felt the pressure of his lips on hers and she was lost. Surrendering herself to the moment was so easy. Everything seemed so different with these strong arms around her and these demanding lips kissing away all her doubts and misgivings.

The sitting room door opened.

'Christ!' said Dick. Mary swung round in horror . . .

Michael was standing in the doorway, the ridiculous figure he cut quite obliterated by the rage which was trembling through his thin frame. He advanced towards them, ashen-faced.

'Get out!' His voice was an intense whisper.

Dick said, 'Now, listen, Michael, you mustn't think that . . .'

'Out of my house,' whispered Michael. 'Out—of—my—house!'

'Please go, Dick,' said Mary.

'But I can't leave you . . .'

'Please . . .'

'All right,' said Dick.

He mustered up what dignity he could and walked to the door. There he paused and turned.

'Michael, I . . .'

'Get out,' said Michael, his voice now stronger. 'And don't ever come through my door again.'

Dick said to her, 'Will you be all right?'

'Yes.'

'You sure?'

'Please. Just go.'

31

Dick gave a last helpless gesture and left the room. In the silence they heard the hall-door close behind him and the the sound of his departing footsteps.

Mary could think of nothing to say or do. She stood there, her head bent, not daring to look at Michael. The anger which was racking him was almost palpable. She could hear his breath coming in little agonised gasps.

She raised her eyes then, genuine fear for his well-being struggling through the shame and dismay which encompassed her.

'Oh Michael . . .'

'Bitch!'

She bent her head again, offering no excuses.

'Whore!'

She said nothing.

There was a pause and the room seemed filled with his shaking anger and his gasping breath.

She made no effort to defend herself as the first blow was struck.

# · CHAPTER THREE ·

# MARKET FORCES

Dinny Byrne was a simple man. He often told his friends that. He had simple desires, simple wants, and made very simple demands of life. He was surrounded by simplicity, from the top of his cloth cap to the soles of his tough leather boots. One of the simplest of his demands was to be allowed sleep on in the morning, especially when he had spent the previous night in the pub, talking to his friends and drinking pints.

He was, therefore, very shocked to have the bedclothes pulled rudely off him and to have his sleep-bleared eyes assaulted by the sight of the angry face of his son.

Miley was roaring at him.

'Get up!'

'What's the matter? What's up?'

'Get up out of bed,' Miley's voice was still a couple of decibels on the wrong side of what could be called decent. 'I've got something to show you.'

Dinny pulled the bedclothes over himself.

'It's too early in the morning. Show me later on.'

The bedclothes were whipped off him again.

'You're getting up now. The day's half wasted.'

Miley walked out of the room, taking the bedclothes with him.

Dinny roared after him, 'Begod, you're looking for a right skelp, do you know that!'

He struggled up from the bed. He was wearing his vest, underpants and socks. His trousers were lying across the back of a chair where he had flung them the night before. With much puffing and panting — Begod, this was no way to treat a Christian! — he put on his cap and fought his way into his trousers, all the while keeping up a stream of abuse against his son.

'Maybe it's time I started showing you who's boss in this house, once and for all . . . big and all as you are.'

Buttoning his flies he walked into the kitchen. It was empty.

'Where are you?' he shouted.

Miley's voice came from outside.

'Out here.'

Dinny found his boots standing near the door.

He pulled them on and stamped out into the sunlight, blinking as the glare attacked his eyes. Miley was standing like the statue of Parnell in O'Connell Street with his hand outstretched, his finger pointing.

'What's these?'

'What's what?'

A cock crew nearby. Dinny found it extremely difficult to focus.

'These here.'

Dinny finally got his eyes moving in harmony and looked at the hens scratching the ground outside the cottage.

'They're like hens,' he said.

Miley snorted, 'I know well they're hens! Do you know how they got here?'

Dinny rubbed his stubbly chin.

'Do you think maybe they strayed?'

Miley glared at him.

'No, hold on,' said Dinny. 'Hold on now. It's coming back to me. Did you count them?'

'There's twelve hens and a cock.'

'Oh that's it so,' said Dinny. 'That explains it. They're ours.'

Miley continued to glare at him.

'I bought them,' said Dinny.

'When?'

'Last night. I got them off a fella called Morrissey.' He paused for effect. 'Wasn't it very decent of him to lave them round?'

'So you were at it again,' said Miley in disgust. 'Down in the pub, talking like T.J. Maher.'

Dinny affected a lofty, dignified tone. 'I got a great bargain of them. . . .'

'Acting the big spender,' growled Miley. 'I only hope you're going to feed them, because I haven't the time.'

'Sure, of course I'll feed them,' said Dinny. 'No bother in the wide world feeding them. And won't we have eggs for the house? And manure for the vegetables? I often heard chicken manure was the best manure of all.'

Miley walked away.

Dinny called after him, 'Where are you going? Did you have your breakfast?'

Miley's voice came from the distance.

'I'll have it later on.'

'I'll get it for you.'

Dinny turned and looked at the hens and at the cock strutting amongst them.

'Don't be letting me down, now,' he said. 'If you don't perform, we'll be rightly in the. . . .'

But days passed and the hens showed a decided disinclination to perform. Dinny cleared a space for them in a shed in the yard and threw an armful or two of straw on the ground. He ran a pole from wall to wall to make a perch for them at night. He fenced off a portion of the yard to make a run. He mixed soggy feed for them and put it into a trough and they devoured it voraciously. No man could have done more to cossett and cajole them. But they simply wouldn't lay eggs.

When Biddy MacDermott saw them, she said, 'They should be laying by now, Dinny.'

'Would you say that?'

He looked at his brood as they fought and argued over the food.

'Do you think,' he asked Biddy, 'that Morrissey saw me coming?'

'Maybe,' said Biddy. 'On the other hand, they look well enough.'

'Why wouldn't they!' said Dinny. 'Ating and tupping all round them and doing nothing for it. I've a good mind to starve them till they see reason.'

But he didn't. He continued to feed them and, as he told Stephen Brennan, to monitor their progress.

'Is that so?' said Stephen.

'Very important,' said Dinny, sipping his pint thoughtfully, 'to monitor their progress.'

'And what progress have they made?' asked Stephen.

'Well, now I'll tell you,' said Dinny. 'Not a whole lot.'

'You should read them a manual on market forces,' said Stephen, grinning at his own joke. 'Give them a lecture on supply and demand. Tell them there's a fierce demand for free-range eggs and that it's up to them to supply them.'

'Do you know what I'm going to say to you, Stephen,' said Dinny. 'You're a great comedian.'

He went home and stared morosely at the hens. They looked fat and sleek after all his care, but they steadfastly refused to lay.

However, a plan was beginning to suggest itself to him. If there was such a demand as Stephen suggested, then the forces of supply would have to be called into action. And if the hens wouldn't supply, then there were those that would.

In the meantime, at the suggestion of Matt Moran, Miley had decided to start a vegetable round. He was so taken up with the idea that he forgot about Dinny and the hens, except when the wind was in the right quarter, or the wrong quarter, depending on the point of view, and wafted unmistakeable evidence of their presence into the cottage.

On the first morning of his round, Miley drove his battered car into the yard, pulling his trailer. He had come from the wholesaler, and the trailer was loaded with fruit and vegetables. As he was walking to the cottage he passed the chicken run. He stopped and sniffed disapprovingly before going on.

Dinny was having his breakfast in the kitchen. He was buttering a piece of soda bread when Miley came in.

'Have you tea made?' asked Miley.

'Just fresh. Do you want a rasher?'

Dinny brought the pan to the table. Miley lifted the rasher out with his fingers, laid it on the piece of bread Dinny had just buttered, and started to eat it. Dinny looked at him, sighed, and began buttering a fresh piece.

'Did you get the stuff?' he asked.

'I did. Are you coming with me?'

'Where?'

'On me rounds.'

'Indeed and I'm not,' said Dinny emphatically.

'I could do with you,' said Miley. 'For chatting up the oul wans.'

Dinny said, 'You won't see me going round the doors like a knacker.'

'Oh fair enough,' said Miley. 'I'd hate to insult you.'

He finished his bread and prepared to leave.

'Tell me something,' he said. 'Do you think maybe you could stoop to putting a bit of fresh straw in the hen-house? Before we're all poisoned.'

'It's a good healthy smell,' said Dinny. 'Nothing the matter with it at all.'

When Miley had departed with his trailer, Dinny rinsed the two cups. Then he went into the bedroom and from under his bed he took a large cardboard box.

He carried the box out of the cottage and over to the hen-house.

'Morning, Dinny,' Biddy called as she passed the cottage on her way to the sprouting shed. 'What's in the box?'

'I'm installing a stereo — to play music for the hens,' said Dinny.

'Ask a stupid question!'

Biddy grinned at him and walked on, shaking her head.

Dinny went into the hen-house. Fowl scattered as he dumped his box on the ground.

'Do you know what I'm going to tell you?' said Dinny. 'I'm going to give you a lesson on market forces. Look here, now, and pay attention.'

He opened the box.

A little later he walked down to the end of the lane where it joined the road. He carried a large square of cardboard in his hand. As he walked he sang a song.

That evening, Miley arrived home from his vegetable round, towing the now empty trailer behind him. He was in good humour. Everything had gone very well. He had met nothing but friendly faces everywhere. People had been willing to buy. He felt that the life of a door to door salesman wasn't half bad.

As he pulled into the yard he saw a strange car parked outside the cottage. A woman was sitting in the car and a man stood beside it.

'Hello,' said Miley, getting out of his car. 'Can I do anything for you?'

'No, thanks,' said the man politely.

There was a little pause. Miley gave a small cough.

'We're here for the eggs,' said the man.

'The eggs?'

'The free-range eggs,' said the man. 'We saw the notice at the gate. . . .'

'Ah yes,' said Miley. 'I saw that meself. It's the other farm you want. MacDermott's.'

He indicated the MacDermott house up the hill.

'No, it's here,' said the stranger. 'Really. The man's gone to get them.'

At that moment Dinny came out of the hen-house carrying a tray full of eggs.

'There we are,' said Dinny. 'Two dozen fresh eggs. Still warm. Are you back, Miley?'

Miley said, 'Where did you . . . ?'

Dinny interrupted him quickly.

'Me son here doesn't like me selling the eggs. He wants me to keep them all for the house. I'll just take them in and wash them for you.'

Miley stared at the eggs on the tray. They were covered with dung and pieces of straw.

'No, please don't bother,' said the man. 'They're fine.'

'Are you sure now?' said Dinny. 'I hate sending you back to Dublin with dirty eggs.'

'It's perfectly all right. Washing won't do them any good at all,' said the man. 'What do I owe you?'

'Three pound, sir,' said Dinny.

'Well worth it,' said the man, producing the money. 'You can't beat a fresh egg.'

Miley stood rooted to the ground as the stranger got into his car and drove away, telling Dinny that he'd be back for more eggs the next week. The woman in the car smiled and waved.

Dinny carefully placed the money in his inside pocket. Miley found his voice.

'Where the hell did you get the eggs?'

'Where does anybody get eggs?' said Dinny. 'The supermarket. Six dozen of size threes. And that's the last of them.'

Miley was shocked.

'And how can you call them free-range?'

'Ah sure, that's all in the mind,' said Dinny complacently.

'But they'll know the minute they taste them!'

'Indeed and they won't,' said Dinny. 'Those two'll go home and boil themselves an egg apiece for their tea, and they'll swear to God they never ate a fresher egg. And they'll keep coming back for more. It's the dung that does it.'

Miley said, 'I was going to ask you about that. . . .'

Dinny went into the henhouse and emerged carrying an empty bucket.

'Sure, that's the whole secret,' he said. 'The bit of dung. I keep them in this, you see, for convenience. The basin of dung's inside. Of course,you just can't dip them in the dung. You've got to make it look natural. Don't overdo it. If you can stick bits of straw to the shell, that's the clincher.'

He started towards the cottage and then turned.

'How did your own stuff go?'

When Mary MacDermott heard about the eggs her reaction was predictable.

'But that's terrible, Dinny. Codding all those poor people.'

'There's nothing poor,' said Dinny, 'about people that can afford one-fifty a dozen for eggs.'

'It's pure fraud and you know it,' said Mary.

'Amn't I entitled to charge for me time and me skill?'

'What skill?'

'The art work on the eggs.'

'That's another thing,' said Mary. 'How can you dip your hands in that stuff?'

'I don't,' said Dinny. 'I did at first, but I gave it up. A bit of Bisto gravy and maybe a drop of mustard. The colour varies, you see. From hen to hen.'

'Will you stop!'

'Then there's the refinements. Little bits of feathers in the mix.'

'And where do you get the feathers?'

'From the hens' backsides. It's good enough for them. Lazy hoors. Pardon the French.'

From then on the hens never looked back. Or if they did, according to Dinny, they saw nothing behind them except supermarket eggs. And he continued to sell his 'free-range' eggs to an ever-widening group of satisfied customers.

Then came an unforgettable day. Biddy arrived at the cottage to find a strange car parked outside the hen-house. There was no sign of the driver. Just at that moment Dinny emerged from the cottage carrying a couple of egg-boxes.

'Have you got a customer?' asked Biddy.

'I have,' said Dinny. 'Inside in the hen-house. I've a new thing now. Pick your own.'

'Pick your own eggs?'

'Like the strawberries,' said Dinny. He lowered his voice. 'I scatter two dozen eggs in the straw,you see, and when people comes I ask them if they'd like to gather their own. Of course they're delighted. I give them a basin and off they go.'

'Do you give them a discount?' asked Biddy.

'Divil the discount.'

'Such an oul fraud,' said Biddy.

'Will you whisht now,' said Dinny. 'It's like a treasure hunt. *They* should be paying *me* extra for the thrill.'

'But you've only twelve hens,' said Biddy. 'How do you explain twenty-four eggs from twelve hens?'

'They don't count the hens,' said Dinny. 'And anyway they think you get eggs from hens like milk from cows, morning and evening.'

A well-dressed woman picked her way out of the hen-house, carrying a basin of eggs.

'Ah there you are, Ma'am,' said Dinny, taking the basin from her. 'Was there two dozen there?'

'Yes, thank you,' said the woman.

Dinny said, 'I'll take them in and wash them for you. . . .'

'Please don't bother,' said the woman. She smiled politely at Biddy, who smiled back equally politely.

Dinny started to put the eggs into the boxes.

'In fact,' said the woman, 'I found twenty-five.'

With an effort, Dinny concealed his surprise. He counted out the eggs.

'Begod, Ma'am, you're right. There's one over. That's three pound, Ma'am.'

When the woman had departed, Biddy burst out laughing.

'You dirty eejit — you planted one too many!'

'I did not,' said Dinny. 'Do you not realise what's after happening? One of them hens is after forgetting herself and laying an egg.'

He held up the egg he had retained.

'This one.'

'How do you know it's that one?' asked Biddy.

'Because it's too clean to be one of mine,' said Dinny. 'That's a genuine free-range egg you're looking at.'

So you'll be able to make an honest man of yourself and sell the real thing from now on.'

'Ah no,' said Dinny. 'You don't want to confuse the people. We'll keep the real ones for the house. Have you got anything to do?'

Biddy shook her head.

'Not a whole lot.'

'I'll go in here,' said Dinny, ' and see if any more hens took the notion. And then you can come into the cottage and I'll boil you an egg.'

# · CHAPTER FOUR ·

# QUE SERA SERA

Ambiguous wasn't a word that Miley Byrne used very often. But he understood what it meant all right. Cows weren't ambiguous. Sheep weren't ambiguous. Even his father's hens weren't ambiguous.

But women were definitely ambiguous.

The night he called to take Biddy MacDermott to the dance and met her sister, Carol, he was very much taken by her. He had never seen anybody quite like her. For one thing, she was pretty. And she was sophisticated. There was the smell of the big city off her. It showed in her clothes and in the way her hair was done. And in the calm way she seemed to know him the minute he walked in the door. Not a bit shy. But then a girl like her didn't need to be shy.

All that night while Biddy and he were at the dance, Miley kept thinking of Carol. He mentioned her a few times to Biddy, just to make conversation, as you might say, but somehow or other the topic never seemed to get very far. Biddy kept seeing people she knew across the ballroom, or it was time to have supper, or she had to go to the ladies' loo to powder her nose. So what he found out about Carol that night wasn't much. She was younger than Biddy. She worked in a bank in Dublin. That was about it. Not a whole lot. But enough to go on.

When they got back to the MacDermott house after the dance, Mary had gone to bed, but Carol was still up. And she looked even prettier than she had done earlier. She had put on a pair of green pyjamas and was curled up on the sofa in the sitting room reading a book. Biddy didn't seem too happy to find her there, but she was probably tired after all the dancing they had done. There was the usual chatter that you'd expect between girls — who had been at the dance, what was the band like, did they give you anything decent for supper?

Miley sat there, looking from one to the other, but mostly at Carol, and smiling any time one of them looked at him. When Biddy went into the kitchen to make a cup of tea, Miley took advantage of the few minutes alone with Carol to ask her if she'd be back down in Glenroe next weekend and, if she would be, would she come out with himself and maybe Matt Moran and Biddy.

41

He didn't really know how he got the courage to ask a girl he had only just met out on a date. It must have had something to do with her manner and the easy friendly way she had with her. It was almost as though she had asked herself.

And he couldn't believe it when she said yes. Just like that.

He remembered how long it had taken him to get Biddy even to go into the pub with him for a drink after the Children's Disco, and he decided that it was fierce how two sisters could be so different in the way they carried on.

Anyway, he was very pleased with himself for being so handy with the women. It only went to show that when a man met the right girl he could be sure of finding the necessary qualities inside himself.

Next day he was flattening drills with the back of a spade when he saw Biddy, on a tractor, harrowing in the field below. He thought to himself what a great friend he had in her. So dependable, so decisive in her work about the farm, the sort of person you want to share things with.

He stuck the spade in the soil and went down to meet her just as she reached the top of the field.

She cut the engine of the tractor, got down and went around to the harrow to examine it. Miley followed her, full of smiles.

'You getting ready for your main crop potatoes?' Miley asked.

Biddy was kneeling at the harrow.

'Yeh.'

'Same as meself,' said Miley. 'I'm putting in onion setts as well. And carrots.'

'You'll be busy,' said Biddy, intent on what she was doing.

Miley put on his most casual air.

'Tell me, did . . . ah . . . did Carol get away all right?'

Without looking up, Biddy said, 'Yeh, she went this morning.'

'Did she?'

Biddy raised a caustic eye.

'Sure, you knew that,' she said tartly. 'Weren't you watching out the window?'

'I was, that's right,' said Miley, laughing at the good of it. Trust Biddy to spot a thing like that. 'She's a nice girl. Really nice.'

'Most men seem to think so.'

'No put-on about her,' said Miley definitively.

There was a pause. He decided it was time to share his good news.

'She's coming down again this next weekend.'

'Oh?'

'As a matter of fact,' said Miley. 'I'm taking her out.' Biddy had her head bent as she adjusted something on the harrow. It took her a moment to reply. Then she said, 'That's nice.'

'Next Saturday,' said Miley. 'I was thinking maybe Matt and yourself could come with us and make up a four. What do you say?'

'I don't know,' said Biddy. She straightened up. 'Damn this thing.'

'Will you be able to come?' asked Miley.

'I said I don't know,' said Biddy crossly. Evidently the harrow was going against her. 'I mightn't be free.'

She turned and walked back towards the house.

Miley followed behind her. He felt deflated that his good news had aroused so little enthusiasm.

And he had trouble with Matt Moran too. Matt didn't want to come on a double date. He didn't have the money to spend. He was going to have enough difficulty trying raise the cash to get his car out of the garage at the weekend.

'We're not all wealthy landowners,' he told Miley.

'I don't mind paying for the night,' said Miley.

But that didn't please Matt at all.

'We've been over that before,' he said. He looked closely at Miley. 'You must be very keen.'

'Well, you have to admit she's a lovely girl,' said Miley.

'I always thought Biddy was just as nice,'

'Ah well,' said Miley, 'Biddy's the best in the world, but . . .'

'They're very different,' said Matt.

'They are,' agreed Miley.

However, Matt did finally raise the money to come on the date and Biddy consented to make up the foursome. On Friday Miley went into Wicklow and got himself a haircut. Dressed up and spruce, he arrived in MacDermott's an hour before the appointed time. Biddy welcomed him, looking much prettier than usual. Miley decided it was the prospect of going out with Matt that had brightened her up.

Matt came dead on eight o'clock. The three of them sat in the sitting room without much to say to each other. Time went by and there was no sign of Carol. Biddy made cups of coffee. They all got gloomier and gloomier.

At ten-fifteen, Miley said, 'She'll hardly come now. Do you think she'll come, Matt?'

'Hard to say, Miley.'

'She hardly will,' said Miley.

'I say we should go on without her,' said Matt. 'Leave a note and she can follow us.'

'I don't know why she couldn't ring,' said Biddy. 'Selfish cow!'

'Maybe she wasn't able,' said Miley reproachfully.

Biddy gave him a very funny look. There was a long pause.

'She'll hardly come now,' said Miley.

'Oh Miley, would you ever shut up!' Biddy snapped at him.

In the heel of the hunt, Biddy made the two men go down to the pub on their own, promising to ring them if Carol turned up. When Miley demurred, she said to him,

'There's no use in wasting the haircut!'

'Are you sure now?' said Miley.

'Just go, will you!'

Carol never arrived. Matt and Miley sat in the pub and had a few drinks and that was the end of that Saturday night.

Miley didn't see much of Biddy during the week. Whenever he caught a glimpse of her she always seemed to be very busy, so that all he got from her was a wave and sometimes not even that. Of course, he was busy himself, what with the vegetable round and the early carrots, but at the same time he sensed that she wasn't pleased about something and he worked it out that it must be the fact that her Saturday night had been messed up.

He made a point of seeking her out. She was walking along her potato drills, when he fell into step with her.

'I haven't seen much of you during the week,' said Miley.

'I was busy.'

'You surely were,' said Miley, looking at the evidence of her work all around them. 'Tell us, were you annoyed last Saturday?'

She professed surprise.

'At what?'

'I'd say you were,' said Miley. 'Matt and me walking out and leaving you on your own. 'Twasn't right.'

They walked in silence a moment.

'Did you hear from Carol since?' asked Miley.

'No.'

'Well, begod I don't think much of her,' said Miley. 'That's telling you straight. Leaving us all sitting there like eejits. I know she's your sister and you'll stand up for her. . . .'

'I'm not standing up for her,' said Biddy.'

'— but there's no excuse at all,' said Miley. 'None.'

At that moment a car passed them on its way up the driveway. They could see Carol in the passenger seat. She waved. They walked up after the car.

'Do you think maybe she mixed up the weekends?' asked Miley.

'Well, I suppose when you think about it. . .'

Bernie stressing a point to Miley while Dinny and Paddy listen attentively.

Mary and Carol MacDermott.

Miley and Biddy enjoy a chat after the children's disco.

Miley tries to persuade Matt and Nuala to make a foursome with himself and Carol.

'Are you up to something, Dinny Byrne?'

A perplexed Miley talking to customers.

Paddy and Miley are surprised at Bernie.

George looks on anxiously while Mary is confident it will work.

Nice surprises and good laughs at the MacDermott-Moran party.

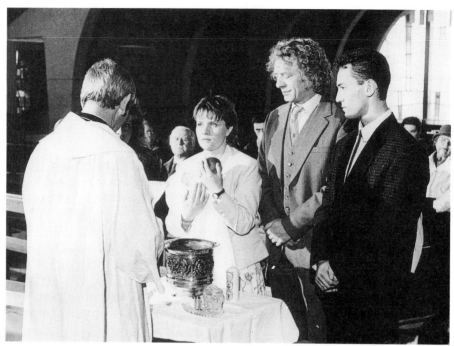

Father Devereux baptises Denise Bridget Byrne.

Dinisheen' doesn't let a whimper out of her.

Biddy said something under her breath that he didn't catch.

By the time they reached the house, the car had already driven away again. Carol was waiting for them and she greeted them effusively.

'We weren't expecting you,' said Biddy.

I know,' said Carol. 'It was just on the spur of the moment. I got the chance of a lift . . .'

She broke off and looked at them both.

'Nothing's the matter, is it?'

Miley knew immediately that they had been blaming her in the wrong. And her explanation proved it. She had been detained in Dublin on business and hadn't been able to get through on the phone. She had sent a message of apology by some friend of hers, who was driving to Glenroe on that Saturday, but evidently he hadn't delivered it.

'Isn't that a fright,' said Miley. 'He didn't bother his head to call. God, he must be a right louser.'

He looked for confirmation from Biddy, but she was looking the other way.

Carol said,' I'm really most awfully sorry.'

'Sure, of course you are,' said Miley.

'I thought we might go out tonight instead.'

Miley was delighted.

'We could of course. I'd have to go and fix it up with Matt. . . .'

'There's the kids' disco,' said Biddy.

'Sure, that's over early,' said Miley. 'We can go after it. Are you game?'

Biddy shrugged.

The four of them went to the disco that night.

From the moment Matt called for them in his car, he and Carol appeared to get along very well together. She sat beside him in the front of the car, leaving Biddy and Miley together in the back. And at the disco, Matt and Carol seemed to be dancing together all the time, while Biddy and Miley sat at a table.

Miley didn't feel happy at all and Biddy too looked pretty glum. All the chatter and laughter came from the other two.

The really low point of the evening came when Matt and Carol returned to the table after a particularly torrid slow set.

'Look, Biddy,' she said. 'Matt's taking me for a run. Do you mind?'

'A run?' said Miley.

'In the car,' Carol beamed at him. 'We'll be back before the end.'

'Maybe,' said Matt.

'If we're not, don't wait,' said Carol.

'Okay,' said Biddy.

Carol forgot to say goodbye to Miley, who sat there dumbfounded.
After a while Miley said to Biddy, 'Do you want to dance?'

'Do *you*?'

'I suppose we might as well,' said Miley.

She looked at him in that peculiar way she had.

'I'm going home,' said Biddy.

'But it's not over yet.'

'It is for *me*.'

Miley followed her towards the door.

'What about Carol? I think we should wait for them.'

Biddy stopped.

'They're not coming back, Miley,' she said, not unkindly.

There was a long moment of silence.

'I suppose they're not,' said Miley.

It was a depressing time for Miley. That same night his trailer was smashed. Then his vegetable round fell to pieces when his customers refused to buy, and he had a run-in with Paddy Maher. Nothing seemed to be going right.

The next time he met Matt Moran, he wasn't in good form. Matt asked him what was wrong.

'It was Carol,' said Miley.

'What about Carol?'

'You moved in,' said Miley. 'I asked her out and you moved in on her.'

Matt was surprised.

'Wait a minute. Are you saying you asked Carol for yourself?'

'Didn't I say it to you!'

'No, you didn't,' said Matt emphatically. 'I assumed all along *I* was to take Carol.'

'Why would you think that?' said Miley crossly.

'Because you and Biddy . . .' said Matt. 'She fancies you.'

'She does not fancy me!'

'And you fancy her.'

'I do not!'

'Take it easy,' said Matt.

Miley had never heard anything so ridiculous in his whole life. He didn't fancy Biddy. You don't 'fancy' a woman like Biddy. Biddy was a friend, almost like another man, though he had to admit that she had moments of ambiguity that no man would ever have.

There was definitely no possibility that she 'fancied' him. Any time he asked her anywhere, even into the pub for a drink, she always had some excuse for not going. She wasn't dressed right, or she had work to do, or she had to go somewhere else, things like that.

Nuala Maher fancied him, though. He could sense that. And it helped him to get over his disappointment about Carol. He even went so far as to have a date with Nuala. Well, it wasn't exactly a date. They were talking in the street one evening when Matt and Carol pulled up in Matt's car.

'Here come the lovebirds,' said Nuala.

It was so obvious that Carol and Matt were in the throes of a hectic romance that it made Miley nearly sick to look at them slobbering over each other, and in a sort of reflex action he asked Nuala to come down to a ballad session in Finn's pub.

And it wasn't a bad night, either.

A few days later he found himself talking to Biddy about the children's disco she ran and he offered to come down again and help.

'Carol's here,' said Biddy suddenly.

'It seems to be a very strong line now, herself and Matt,' said Miley.

'Carol's lines are always strong,' said Biddy. 'While they last.'

Miley grew confidential.

'I might as well tell you, Biddy,' he said, 'I was keen on her meself.'

'You're joking,' said Biddy in a very flat voice.

'It's a fact,' said Miley. 'I don't mind telling you I was hard hit when she went off with Matt. Where do you think I went wrong?'

'Why are you asking me?' said Biddy coldly.

'Well . . . because you know Carol best and . . .'

'Is it for future reference?' said Biddy with more heat in her voice. 'I mean, you weren't long consoling yourself with Nuala Maher.'

'Who told you that I . . .'

Biddy was now firing on all cylinders.

'Carol told me. She thought it was a great laugh. Well, I didn't! You can moon around Carol or Nuala or any other juvenile delinquent you fancy, but don't come to me for sympathy when you get ditched!'

And she stamped off.

'Biddy', Miley called after her. 'Will I call for you this evening? For the kids' disco?'

'Go on your own,' she shouted back at him. 'You're more on *their* wavelength than I am!'

There was no doubt that women were a queer class of an animal.

So he went to the kids' disco on his own. And when it was over and the last of the children had just gone home, who came in but Nuala Maher. She was all dressed up in something very colourful, and she was wearing a lot of lipstick and big shiny earrings.

Before Miley knew where he was she had put a record on the turntable.

She turned to Miley.

'Come on.'

He hesitated.

'Ah, come on,' she repeated. 'Sure there's nobody to see you.'

But of course it wasn't Miley's week. While they were dancing, Nuala with her arms around Miley's neck, Paddy Maher suddenly came into the disco. He had come down on Dinny's suggestion to patch things up with Miley, but the sight of his sister in this 'blow-in's' arms, added to the few pints he had consumed upstairs in the pub, proved too much for him.

'What do you think you're doing messing with my sister?'

The accusation was so unfair that Miley was stung into unaccustomed retaliation.

'Oh you're a very tough man, aren't you? You're well able to frighten women. . . .'

'All right,' shouted Paddy. 'Outside!'

However, it didn't quite come to pistols at dawn. The sound of their raised voices brought people down from the pub and no actual blows were struck. But they were both barred from the Molly Malone.

Miley got scant sympathy from his father the next day.

'What the divil is worrying you — apart from losing the heifer?' asked Dinny.

'You think you're annoying me, don't you?' said Miley. 'Calling Carol a heifer.'

'Well, something's annoying you.'

'Amn't I after losing me livelihood? And getting barred from the pub?' Miley paused for breath. 'And the cabbage isn't looking too good either.'

'Oh holy God,' said Dinny. 'You're a right misery. Why don't you go out somewhere this evening and cheer yourself up.'

'Nobody to go with.'

'It's a pity about you,' said Dinny. 'Couldn't you ask Biddy?'

Miley gave a bitter laugh.

'Biddy doesn't go out.'

'She doesn't go because she's not asked,' said Dinny.

They both looked out the window. They could see Biddy hard at work in her potato field.

'What'll I do if she says no?'

'You could try hanging yourself,' said Dinny.

Miley thought that was a bit over the top. He scowled at his father and went out.

Biddy looked up when she noticed him standing near her.

'Howrya,' said Miley.

'Howrya.'

'I wanted to ask you something,' said Miley.

Just then he spotted the figure of Dinny walking from the cottage in the direction of the MacDermott home.

'Do you see him!' said Miley. 'I told him we had the carrots to weed. And look at him sneaking off.'

'You said you had something to ask me,' said Biddy.

'Oh aye. 'Twasn't much really. I just wondered, like, I don't suppose you're interested in the pictures at all?'

'Yeh, I like the pictures,' said Biddy. 'I don't often go. . . .'

She resumed working.

'I'm the same,' said Miley. 'I was kind away wondering if you'd be interested in going to the pictures.'

'When?'

'This evening. I hear it's good.'

'What is it?'

'I don't know. But I hear it's good.'

'I wouldn't mind,' said Biddy.

'I'll call for you about half-six.'

She nodded. Miley turned away.

'Just one thing,' said Biddy.

He looked at her.

'If you mention Carol,' said Biddy, 'I'm going home.'

'Sure, why would I mention Carol?'

She turned her back to him and moved down the field.

Miley wondered what made her think he'd mention Carol. There was no doubt that she was an ambiguous person. But good company all the same. He wasn't sure whether he enjoyed the picture or not ( he found it most peculiar) but he enjoyed the night. Going to the pictures with a friend like Biddy was a nice easy way to pass an evening. He decided that it was the sort of thing he should do more often.

And, as the weeks and months went by, things started to get better for him. Paddy Maher came and made it up and the two of them divided the territory and the customers between them. And Miley got a real bargain of a van from Dick Moran. He felt that he was really going to succeed at the vegetable round after all.

Of course, there was the unpleasant happening in MacDermott's house when Biddy and himself found Mary beaten and unconscious. But even that brought Biddy closer to him, to the point where she confided in him that the cuplrit was her own father, who had found her mother and Dick Moran kissing in the sitting room.

So one night, when they returned from the kids' disco and after he had thanked her for saving the greater portion of his carrot crop (she was always looking after himself and his father and correcting their agricultural mistakes) Miley raised a topic he had been thinking about for some time.

'There was something I wanted to say to you.'

'Yes?' said Biddy.

'Maybe I shouldn't say it,' said Miley.

'Force yourself.'

'You heard me talking about buying the new van. Would you fancy going into partnership?'

She turned herself round and looked at him.

'On the vegetable round,' said Miley.

'OK,' said Biddy.

'What do you mean, OK?'

'I mean I'll do it,' said Biddy.

'Begod, you were very quick deciding.'

'I thought about it before now,' said Biddy. 'And I'll pay my share of the van tomorrow.'

'You will not!' said Miley.

But of course she did. And not only that. She also brought to the operation a degree of organization that amazed Miley. She produced a book with pages devoted to Sales Projections and Product Analysis. He couldn't immediately see what that had to do with selling a few vegetables from door to door, but she pointed out that it was a business they were in together and that running a business involved doing things in a business-like way. And even if it were only a few vegetables today who knew how many it would be in the future.

There was no doubt that he had made the right decision in asking her to be his partner.

And then she started to go around with Des Brennan, Stephen's son, who ran the garage in Glenroe. Des's car began to arrive at the MacDermott house and Miley watched Biddy going off in it.

He told himself that she was entitled to go out with anyone she chose. It wasn't any of his business really. And when Matt Moran passed some remark about not letting Des 'wipe his eye', Miley found himself getting a bit hot about it.

'Nobody's wiping *my* eye,' he told Matt. 'My eye's not so aisy wiped.'

But people wouldn't mind their own business. Even Mary MacDermott couldn't keep her mouth shut, but she had to go and say something about Biddy's 'getting tired of waiting'.

Waiting for what? he asked himself. He had asked Biddy on more than one occasion to go out with him, but she always seemed to have a date nowadays.

Des Brennan had even started to go to the children's disco to lend Biddy a hand. And when Biddy told him that she'd be starting the spuds the following day and Miley offered to check over the digger for her, he found that Des had already done it.

He began to feel a bit redundant.

But then a peculiar thing happened. Biddy actually asked him to take her out.

She had fallen and hurt her arm, but he didn't think that that had really anything to do with the invitation. There was a party on in Moran's that evening and they had both decided that they didn't want to go.

And then Biddy suddenly said, 'Will you take me out then?'

Miley looked at her.

'What about Des?' he asked.

'You can take Des out too, if you want to,' Biddy grinned at him.

'Begod' said Miley, highly pleased, 'but you've got very comical lately!'

That evening, as they were driving along, the car broke down. Miley swore at it, not that that did any good. Biddy suggested that he ought to get a new one, and that Des might be able to fix him up.

'Des!' snorted Miley. 'I'm sick and tired hearing about Des!'

'Des was nothing,' said Biddy. 'Just somebody to go out with. And anyway he's moved on to Nuala Maher.'

'Are you upset?'

'I'm relieved, if you want to know,' said Biddy. 'I was bored out of my mind listening to him talking about transverse engines and over-head camshafts.'

There was silence while Miley digested this.

Then Biddy said, 'Come here to me.'

And before he knew where he was she leaned over and kissed him. Right full on the mouth.

When she drew back he could only stare at her.

'If you say one word about spring onions,' said Biddy, 'I think I'll kill you!'

From then on things were very comfortable. They went out regularly together and everybody in the village accepted that they were a pair.

Miley was very happy about it. They had their little differences from time to time, but nothing very serious. He felt as if he could go on like this forever.

Then one evening when he called for Biddy to take her down to the pub, Mary left him in the kitchen with Michael MacDermott while she went to fetch her daughter. Michael was reading the local paper. Miley sat down across the table from him and tried to make conversation, but managed to extract no more than a few grunts.

Then Michael suddenly put the paper down and looked straight into his face.

'Are you going out with Biddy?' he asked.

'That's right,' said Miley.

'Where are you bringing her?'

'The pub.'

'Is that the only place you ever bring her?'

'Ah no,' said Miley. 'Sometimes I bring her to the pictures. Or the odd dance. But it's mostly the pub.'

'You wouldn't have brought a young girl to the pub in my day,' said Michael.

Miley nodded. Then he shook his head. Then he nodded again.

'Tell us this now,' said Michael. 'Have you serious intentions towards Biddy, or are you only poodlefakin' about?'

Miley didn't quite know what to say.

'Ah . . . well, I'm very fond of her.'

'I didn't ask you that,' said Michael.

'Well, like,' said Miley, 'I've great respect for her. But sure, I only know her for a year and a half. 'Tis early days.'

'You've no money ayther,' said Michael.

'Well, I haven't a lot at the moment,' said Miley. 'But I've great prospects. And I owe nothing.'

'I always thought she'd do better for herself,'said Michael. 'But she's twenty-five now. She can't be too choosy.'

'No,' agreed Miley.

'I'd like to see Biddy settled,' said Michael. 'Do you understand me?'

'Oh I do,' said Miley. 'I surely do.'

He surely *did* know what Michael was on about. But knowing something and acting on it were two different things entirely.

Not that there wasn't enough marriage in the air in Glenroe just then. Nuala and Des arrived home from England with the knot well and truly tied. And then Paddy Maher and his girl, Bernie Quinn, got an offer of an opportunity to start their own business in Great Yarmouth and decided to go for it. This meant bringing their wedding plans forward.

Oh yes, there was marriage in the air all right.

And then Michael MacDermott died.

Although he was an old man, he was a very active one, and the end came suddenly one day up in the top field among his cattle. For him it was perhaps the easiest way out of the world; for Mary it was a heartbreak because of her guilt over the affaire with Dick Moran.

Biddy too was very broken up about it. She clung to Miley after the funeral and, in one way,they had never been closer. But it definitely pushed the idea of marriage off the stage for the time being. Damn it, a man couldn't go courting a girl and ask her to give up grieving for her father and to start thinking about things like marriage that could always wait.

Besides, in Michael's will she was left the whole farm and everything on it. Whatever else Michael had owned was left to Mary, with the proviso that she look after Carol. There was generally thought to be a large amount of money involved, though how large nobody really knew, apart from the solicitor and the family, that is. Dinny was very curious about it and spent a lot of time trying to find out just how much Mary had inherited. He talked such a lot about this money that he made Miley nervous and edgy.

Biddy was still his partner, of course. They were going to start growing mushrooms together. But now she was a rich partner, far richer than he was. That was all right as far as the business went. But it sort of made anything else between them more unlikely than ever.

Miley thought again about what Michael had said to him, that he had always hoped 'that Biddy would do better for herself'. Those were the very words he had used. Do better. If the truth were told she couldn't do much worse than somebody like himself.

So the best thing was to wait. And when his father made some remark about courting the girl properly, Miley snapped back at him,

'When I start coortin' I'll need no help from you!'

Biddy's sickness came suddenly and dramatically.

One minute she seemed as fit and well as ever she was, the next minute she was whisked off to hospital.

And her going made the whole place desolate. Not just the farm, but all Glenroe itself.

Mary went with her to the hospital and Dinny and Miley were left behind like a couple of spare parts. They remained in the MacDermott house where they could be near a telephone. But Mary didn't come back that night, nor did she telephone. Anything might be happening. Miley found it impossible to sleep. He got up stiff and sore from the easy chair where he had tried to make himself comfortable. Dinny was snoring away on the sofa.

Miley walked out into the cold dawn. He had never seen the countryside look so dreary. The village of Glenroe was like an empty tomb. He kept thinking of all the things he had been on the point of saying, but had never said. It was if he had an immense, mighty hole in his heart.

When Mary finally returned with the news that it was meningitis, that was some little comfort. Despite the visions of terror associated with the word, it was somehow easier to have a name put on the nameless, to have the enemy identified and capable of being dealt with.

Mary took him with her the next time she visited the hospital. They sat by the bed, looking at the pale and unconscious Biddy as she lay there, all the competent assurance drained out of her small body, her eyes closed, her breath shallow and delicate. There were tubes sticking out of her, cold bottles with strange fluids in them.

One day he was there alone, sitting quietly, when he was so moved that he took her hand in his and leaned over her.

'Biddy?' he said. 'Can you hear me?'

There was no change in her appearance, nor in her regular quiet breathing.

'Listen to me,' said Miley. 'Can you hear me? Once you get out of this place, I'm never letting you out of my sight again.'

Was there a slight, flickering movement of her fingers in his hand? He couldn't be sure.

A few days later she suddenly turned the corner. When the news reached Glenroe, smiles began to appear on the faces of Mary and Dinny and Miley. Voices were raised again and they found time for jokes and chatter. It was truly amazing what one bit of good news could do for everything.

When she finally came home, still pale and weak, but better, he fetched her with Mary in the car. And the minute she reached the place she had to get out and look at the potatoes.

'Time they were lifted,' she said accusingly to Miley.

'Sure I know,' said Miley. 'And haven't I got everything ready to start in the morning.'

But all sorts of things still remained to be done. And she told him so, without putting a tooth in it.

Miley was very confused. His relief was immense, but he felt such a useless lump, not able to do anything right on his own without this little butty bit of a girl to direct him and scold him.

When she asked him if he remembered saying something to her in the hospital about not letting her out of his sight again, he found himself telling her that he didn't remember.

'Now, I'm not saying that I didn't say it,' he told her. 'If you say I said it I probably did say it.'

He paused and walked around the room.

'Are you sure it was me?'

'Of course it was you!' she snapped back at him.

Then she dropped the bombshell. She was still weak and spent a lot of time sitting on the sofa, looking delicate and pretty, so when she told him that she was thinking of taking a break he immediately agreed that of course she should. But when she said two years, he nearly fell out of his standing.

'Two years!!'

'Carol's out in Bahrain,' said Biddy, careful not to look him straight in the eye. 'I'll go out and spend time with her, see a bit of the world. I've never been anywhere in my life. Never even been out of Ireland. It may be my last chance.'

Miley could only sit there nodding stupidly.

'Can you think of anything to keep me here?' she asked.

But he couldn't. He was too confused. Well, he *could*, but he wasn't able to put it into words.

She had plenty of money now. She could do what she wanted.

The next day Miley woke up in very bad humour.

He fought with his father for not having given a hand with lifting the spuds the day before and he absolutely refused to let Dinny come up to see Biddy with him. He even refused to give him a lift into the village. It was a black day in his life, even blacker in some ways than the time she had been fighting for her life in the hospital.

He found George Manning in the pub eating a meagre lunch. George lived in the big house at Sloe Hill, where his family had lived for generations, lording it over the local peasantry. George, however, lorded it over nobody. For one thing, he was too nice a man to do anything of the sort. For another, he had no money, merely a large, expensive, inherited house to keep.

He was a naturalist by inclination and an illustrator of nature books by profession. Sometimes, when he got commissions, he spent months away in foreign parts, observing and drawing the local flora and fauna. When he was, as now, 'resting' between commissions, he drifted rather aimlessly around Glenroe, where he was universally liked and even considered one of themselves.

Miley sat himself down beside George. George politely put aside the newspaper he had been reading and prepared himself for listening. He could read the signs.

'Did you ever think of getting married, George?' Miley asked.

George admitted that the thought had crossed his mind once or twice, but that nothing tangible had ever come of it.

'*I'm* thinking of it,' said Miley.

'Ah,' said George.

'I've made me mind up,' said Miley. 'I think.'

He leaned forward confidentially.

'It's Biddy MacDermott.'

'I rather thought it might be,' said George.

'What I want to know is, how do I go about it,' said Miley. 'I mean, what do I say?'

'Ah,' said George again. 'I presume the young lady knows what's coming?'

'Oh lord, no,' said Miley. 'No, no. Sure, I haven't as much as mentioned it.'

'Nevertheless . . .' George began. Then he looked at Miley's expression and decided not to pursue that particular line.

'Well,' said George, 'you should speak your mind. Look her straight in the eye. And say something like . . . ah . . . "Look here, old girl, you and I have been keeping company for quite a long time and neither of us is getting any younger. So why don't we stop all this nonsense and tie the old knot?"'

Miley thought he had never heard anything so concise and to the point.

'Tie the knot,' he said admiringly. 'Begod, George, I think you've hit it right on the head.'

He bought George a drink to show his gratitude and went home with the words ringing around in his brain.

Biddy was languishing on the sofa watching the television. When Miley entered the sitting room, she motioned him to silence. He stood looking at her. Then he sat down. Then he immediately stood up again and switched off the set.

'Hey!' said Biddy indignantly.

'I've got something in particular I want to say to you. . . .' Miley began.

'Well, I've got a few things I want to say to you,' said Biddy.

And there he was standing like a post, listening to a long lecture about the state of the vegetables in the polythene tunnel and what needed to be done with the lettuce, the tomatoes, the early bunching carrots and the indoor strawberries. He kept nodding and agreeing until he could take no more. He turned and walked out of the room.

'Where are you going?' asked Biddy.

'I'm going to the toilet.'

But he didn't want to go to the toilet. He turned and came back.

'I don't want to go to the toilet at all at all.'

'Well, don't,' said Biddy. 'Sit down.'

'I will not sit down!' said Miley defiantly. 'I came in here this evening with something important to say to you and you wouldn't let me get a word in edgeways. Going on about tomatoes and early bunching strawberries! And a whole lot of other things that don't matter a damn.'

There was a pause. She was looking at him wide-eyed.

'Well, go on,' she said.

'Well,' said Miley. 'Remember the time you were lying above in the hospital half-conscious and I said that I was never going to let you out of my sight again. . . .'

'You said you didn't remember.'

'Well, I do remember. And I meant it.'

There was another pause.

'But what difference does it make now,' said Miley.

'Why shouldn't it make a difference?'

There was something very appealing about the expression on her face.

'You're running off to Katmandu and South America and . . .'

'I never said I was going. . . .'

'Yes, you did, and you needn't deny it!'

He stood there, not looking at her. After a moment she said,

'Is that all you wanted to say?'

'No, there was more.'

He paused again, trying to remember what George had told him to say. Biddy waited.

'Maybe I'm wasting my time,' said Miley, 'but I'm going to say it anyway. What I'm going to say is . . . well, we've been knocking around together for along time now. And neither of us are getting any younger. So why don't we . . . why don't we stop all this cod-acting and tie the oul knot?'

It was out now and there was no going back.

Biddy said in a little voice, 'You mean . . . ?'

'You know right well what I mean.'

'I think I do.'

But she said nothing more. He didn't know what to do, or where to look, or where to put his hands. For what seemed like a hundred years he stood there feeling stupider every minute. Finally he sat down on the sofa beside her.

'Well,' said Miley, looking her straight in the eye. 'What's your answer?'

Biddy suddenly began to smile.

'You took your time.'

# · CHAPTER FIVE ·

# THE ROCKY ROAD TO ROME

'Here, let me help,' said Dick Moran.

He cleared dirty dishes out of the way and made a space on the kitchen table. With a sigh, Mary MacDermott put down the laden tray.

'Thanks, Dick,' she said.

There was crockery everywhere about the room. Plates were piled in the sink, glasses with the dregs of stout and sherry and whiskey in them stood along the worktop, used teacups occupied every available inch of table space.

'It's quite a mess.'

'Mm.'

He put his hands on her shoulders and looked into her face.

'How do you feel?'

'Tired.'

She managed a wan little smile.

'There's a terrible mob out there,' said Dick.

'Oh I don't mind,' said Mary. 'They're all friends. And it's good to keep busy.'

They stood a moment in silence. From the sitting room came the chatter of voices and now, increasingly, the opening and closing of the hall-door.

'I think they're starting to leave,' said Dick.

He wanted to take her in his arms and hold her tightly, but he knew that she would resist. It wasn't the time or the place for any show of affection beyond what was required of a friend at a time of bereavement.

'Did you have any idea?' he asked. 'Any warning?'

Her eyes filled with tears.

'No,' she said. 'There was the pneumonia . . . but that was nearly a year ago. Perhaps it affected his heart.'

Dick nodded. Michael had been so old that almost any illness could have been a terminal one.

'I think he knew,' said Mary.

'Why do you say that?'

'He started to worry about things,' she said, her face clouding at the memory. 'The children. He kept saying he wanted to see them settled. And he worried about me too. He said such strange things. Things that weren't like him at all.'

'What things?'

She looked straight into his eyes.

'He said he'd taken my youth.'

Dick shook his head. His hands tightened on her shoulders.

'He didn't do that, Mary. You've plenty left.'

He wanted to add that there was lots of time left for them to share. But again he held his tongue. He was used to holding his tongue when the situation demanded it.

He drove home that night in a determined mood. He wanted Mary MacDermott, there was no doubt about that. In a life that had seen an unsuccessful marriage and a few transient affaires, Mary stood out as a shining light, the one woman of worth he had ever taken a fancy to. And what he felt for her was much more than a fancy.

And he knew that she wanted him too. She had said so often enough, even after that disastrous night when Michael had caught them together and had vented his anger on Mary in the only way he knew how. Even after that, things had started to return gradually to what they had been before.

Now Michael was dead. And Ruth had divorced Dick. In theory, at any rate, there should be nothing but calm seas and plain sailing from now on.

But Dick had been involved in too many business deals not to be aware that the moment you thought you were safely home in port was the moment you ran aground on some unexpected sandbank.

He must play his cards carefully. Mary was not to be rushed.

But perhaps she might be tempted.

When he found out, by reading a confidential file in the office of his son, Paul, that George Manning was thinking of selling Sloe Hill, Dick decided to put in a bid for the property. He felt no qualms about reading the confidential files of others when there was something to be discovered that might be useful to himself. Anyway, Paul was his son. Dick had paid for his education and set him up in his bright new solicitor's office, and he expected to be given little snippets of profitable information every now and again. When Paul had a fit of the principles and started to go on about client confidentiality, Dick solved the problem by simply examining the files in his son's absence.

On his way up to Sloe Hill, he met Dinny Byrne in the street. The talk turned to Biddy and Miley and where they intended to live after their marriage.

'I wouldn't say there was any problem about that,' said Dinny.

'Mary's house?'

'Sure, where else.'

'And what about Mary?' asked Dick, a bit annoyed at the man's insensitivity.

'Isn't there room for the three of them?'

'Well, I don't know,' said Dick. 'That sort of arrangement doesn't always work out.'

But Dinny could see no difficulty.

'A man about the place'll be no harm. He nearly lives there, anyway.'

Dick grunted.

As they were parting, Dinny suddenly said,

'Mary's a fine woman, Dick.'

'She deserves a fine man,' agreed Dick.

'She does, she does,' said Dinny. 'But you hang in anyway, Dick. She might settle for less.'

'Do you know, Dinny,' said Dick. 'If anybody else said that to me, I'd be annoyed.'

'But sure, who else would say it to you?'

True, thought Dick, as he drove away. Dinny was a man apart in Glenroe. And the cute old goat had crossed Dick on more than one occasion in the past. Dick allowed himself a smile at the memory.

He found George pinning up holly in the sitting room in Sloe Hill.

'Ah Dick, how nice,' said George in his usual amiable fashion. 'Please come in. What would you like to drink?'

'Whiskey?'

George was at the drinks table on which stood a lone bottle of sherry.

'Er . . . we seem to be out of whiskey.'

'Drop of gin, then.'

'Er . . .' said George in evident distress.

'Anything at all, George,' said Dick.

'Sherry?

'Fine,' said Dick.

When he had sipped his sherry, Dick said,

'Beautiful house. I hear you may be selling?'

The temperature of George's welcome fell several degrees. No, he hadn't given any such instructions and he couldn't for the life of him imagine where Dick had heard the rumour.

'But if you *were* selling . . . you'd be ready to listen to offers?'

'Do you mean there's a prospective buyer?'

Dick smiled at him.

'You?' asked George, in evident surprise.

'Why not?'

'Well,' said George, 'I shouldn't have thought of it as your cup of tea.'

'Above my station?' said Dick with an edge to his voice.

'Your words, Dick, not mine,' said George.

But the phrase rankled. Dammit, he had as much right as anyone to live in a house like that. For one thing, he could afford to pay for it. George had it for nothing and couldn't afford even a glass of whiskey for a guest.

And then the bumbling squire took it out on Paul for divulging confidential information. He withdrew all his legal affairs from Paul's care. And, of course, Paul vented his self-righteous indignation on his father.

'You've been reading my confidential files!' he shouted at Dick.

'Which particular confidential files?'

'George Manning's.'

'Was that confidential?'

Paul was really angry.

'Everything in here is confidential! I could have been struck off.'

'Don't talk rubbish, Paul! I don't want to hear any more.'

Dick felt he was getting a lot of undeserved censure merely for trying to impress Mary MacDermott and he wasn't prepared to stand and listen to his son lecturing him.

A few days after Christmas he drove out to MacDermott's. He brought with him a large bunch of flowers.

Mary and Biddy were standing outside the house when he arrived. The moment they saw the flowers, the two of them started to laugh.

'What's the joke?' asked Dick.

'Nothing,' Mary giggled. 'They're lovely.'

Biddy went away still laughing.

'Is my shirt tail out?' said Dick, a little nettled.

'No, honestly, it's nothing,' said Mary. 'Biddy was just saying the she wished someone would bring her a bunch of flowers, and the next minute you drove up.'

'I've put in an offer for George's place,' said Dick.

Mary nodded.

'You don't seem surprised,' he said.

'I had the impression you were interested. And when I heard there was another offer on top of the Monsignor's . . .'

'Yes,' said Dick. 'It was me.'

'It's a big place,' said Mary. 'Are you thinking of starting a hotel?'

'You know what I'm thinking, Mary. I don't have to spell it out.'

'I'd far rather you *did* spell it out.'

'All right,' said Dick. 'In simple language, I think we should get married.'

She opened her mouth to speak, but he carried on,

'Not now, not tomorrow. No pressure.'

'How can you say 'no pressure'! Going around buying manor houses!'

'I could really make something of that place,' said Dick earnestly. 'I've talked to an interior architect. He's working on it already.'

'Oh don't, Dick,' said Mary. 'It's just not on.'

'Why not?'

She didn't answer.

'Is it Ruth?'

She looked away from him.

'Listen,' said Dick. 'That's been over a long time. The divorce is final. I have the papers.'

Mary said slowly, 'As far as I'm concerned, you and Ruth are still married.'

'You really believe that?' said Dick. 'We've lived separate lives for eleven years, she has a legal divorce and a new husband . . . and you believe we're still married?'

'Yes,' said Mary.

He exhaled sharply with impatience.

'Just how long is it going to take? Till death us do part?'

'I'm sorry, Dick.'

'Sorry!'

'Even if we *could* get married,' said Mary, 'how could we live in Sloe Hill . . . with the whole village talking about us?'

He was getting angry now.

'Do you mean that if people didn't know about us, it would be all right?'

'No, I don't.'

'We can't get married because that's a sin!' Dick was now in full flight. 'But the odd dirty weekend's all right, provided nobody finds out!'

Mary was now angry herself.

'Stop it, Dick . . . !'

'That's the truth of it, isn't it?' he interrupted her. 'It's not a moral thing at all. It's what the neighbours think!'

'I never knew you could be so vicious,' said Mary.

'And I never knew you could be so shallow!' he snapped back at her.

He stamped back to his car. As he started the engine, the bunch of flowers came flying in through the open window. He got one glimpse of Mary's angry face before he revved the engine and shrieked off.

He stormed back to the office and told Paul and Matt that he wanted them both out of the place. It was a pretty futile gesture, but it made him feel better. He swung about in his swivel chair and glowered at the walls.

After a while he picked up the phone and rang Father Devereux. But there was no news about the annulment proceedings. The priest told him, as he had told him so many times before, that these things take time.

Time wasted on mumbo-jumbo, thought Dick, as he put down the phone. Left to himself, he wouldn't have bothered about asking anyone's permission to remarry, provided he could do it within the law. And he would even have flouted the law, provided the penalties weren't too heavy.

But not with Mary. She was Catholic. She believed in sin and that marriages were made in heaven. She might slip from time to time, but they were only temporary misdemeanours, to be confessed and atoned for in the Sacrament of Penance. She would never dream of basing her whole life on what she considered a sinful union.

He often asked himself how he had managed to get mixed up with such a believer in the traditional values of a religion he himself had long since ceased to practise in any meaningful way. But there it was. A man didn't choose to fall in love with a particular woman. It just happened. And he was stuck with it.

He failed to buy Sloe Hill. George withdrew the place from auction and both of the prospective buyers had to go away empty-handed. Dick, however, managed to salvage some benefit from the proceedings by finding another house for the Monsignor and his community of nuns.

He went out to see Mary.

She received him coolly, but brought him in and gave him a drink.

'I didn't get to talk to you yesterday,' said Dick. 'At the auction.'

'I had to hurry off. Were you disappointed?'

'Not really. You win some and you lose some. It wasn't a total loss. George is talking to me again. I think I found a place for Father Jim. And Dinny sold me a dog.'

Mary smiled.

'That's nice.'

'I like to see you smiling,' said Dick. 'You don't do it often enough lately.'

'I'm sorry we fought, Dick,' said Mary. 'I don't know why we do.'

'It seems simple enough. We don't want the same things.'

'I think we do,' said Mary.

She was seated on the settee, staring into the fire. He went and sat beside her.

He began, 'Are you saying . . .'

'I'm not saying anything, Dick,' she said. 'Please don't talk about it. We'll only fight again.'

He put his arm around her and they sat in silence awhile.

Then Mary said, 'Would you really have bought the house?'

'Oh yes.'

'But why?'

'To show you that I meant what I said,' said Dick.

Mary smiled again.

'You don't have to prove it,' she said gently and kissed him. 'You just have to give me time.'

Everybody wanted his time. The Catholic Church. The woman he loved. And Dick Moran wasn't used to being kept waiting. When he wanted something his usual practice was to go out and get it immediately, and he was never very particular about the methods he used.

It was in pursuance of this admirable goal that he told Paul and Matt that he wanted them out of the office, because he was taking a partner.

'It's an existing agency with a very healthy business in South County Dublin. I supply an office here; they give me one in Dublin. So I'm afraid you both have to go.'

They weren't pleased, of course. But he wasn't in the business of pleasing anyone — except Mary MacDermott.

On the day the new partner arrived, Matt came in from the Greystones office which he was now managing on his own.

'Paul asked me to pick up something,' said Matt. 'That's if you don't mind.'

'No, no,' said Dick. 'But maybe you should knock. The new partner's moved in.'

'Oh I see,' said Matt. 'I'll come back again.'

'Go on in. You have to meet sometime.'

'What's he like?' asked Matt.

'You see one Estate Agent, you've seen them all,' said Dick.

But Matt hadn't often seen an Estate Agent like the beautiful and sophisticated young lady who rose from her desk to greet him.

'Hello,' she said. 'Are you Paul?'

'Matt,' said Matt.

'Ah, then we're partners. I'm Barbara Downes.'

Matt wondered vaguely what his father was up to.

What Dick was up to was quite simple. Barbara's stay in Glenroe wouldn't last longer than a couple of weeks. He had chosen to go into partnership with her because she ran an efficient business; her physical appearance was no more than an added bonus. But being a man who was always ready to make use of whatever, or whomever, might come along to help him further his own plans, he decided that a visit to Mary MacDermott with a beautiful young woman in tow would do his cause no harm at all. So he arrived out at the MacDermott house with Barbara that same day. They came unannounced and surprised Mary in her working-clothes, a scarf around her head and a pair of rubber gloves on her hands. For Mary it was a near disaster, but Dick was pleased with the effect the visit caused.

A couple of days later it bore fruit when Mary asked Barbara and himself out to dinner. It was a good meal. Auntie Florrie was there, of course, and Father Devereux dropped in, but Dick was getting all sorts of good vibes from Mary. During the course of the evening, when she was carrying out some dishes, he opened the door for her and then followed her into the kitchen.

'You're looking very nice tonight,' he said.

'A little better than the last time,' Mary admitted with a wry smile.

He put his arms around her and she didn't resist.

'She's quite attractive,' said Mary.

'Mm.'

'And successful,' said Mary. 'For someone so . . . comparatively young.'

Dick grinned.

'Oh I don't know. She's not that much younger than you.'

When she looked at him reproachfully, he added,

'You asked for that.'

He kissed her.

'She's my business partner, Mary. That's all.'

It was a most satisfactory evening. And when Barbara later on accused him of using her to strengthen his position with Mary, he didn't deny it.

After Mass the following Sunday, they went for a walk in the woods.

'I spoke to Father Devereux about the annulment,' said Dick.

'Had he any news?'

'Not really,' said Dick. 'But suppose, for the sake of argument, that it came through . . .'

Mary walked a little in silence before she replied.

'I just don't know. I couldn't make any promises, Dick.'

'All right, no promises,' said Dick. 'But I *would* like an agreement.'

'That's the same thing. . . .'

'An agreement not to hide things. Not to mind being seen together. Not to care if the whole parish is looking at us.'

'All right,' said Mary finally. 'Within reason.'

'Good,' said Dick. 'That's progress. For a start we can have dinner one night next week. In Dublin.'

'Yes,' said Mary.

'Well, that was easier than I expected,' said Dick. 'You won't want Florrie as a chaperone?'

Mary laughed.

'You don't bring Barbara Downes, I won't bring Auntie Florrie.'

The dinner in Dublin was very successful. Everything was so much better than it had been on the disappointing weekend in Cork. That night Mary stayed in Moran's and the following morning startled George Manning by appearing on the doorstep in her dressing gown just as he was about to knock on the door. It was an embarrassment for both of them.

But the relationship between Dick and Mary blossomed from then on. When Miley and Biddy got married and Mary wished to move out into a house of her own, it was Dick who found it for her and who got it for a very good price by the simple expedient of contributing £15,000 of his own money, unknown to Mary. She took Auntie Florrie to live with her and Biddy and Miley settled down in the old MacDermott home.

The only problem, as far as Dick was concerned, was that they had to snatch their time together how and where and when they could. On most occasions they kissed goodbye at Mary's door in the manner of a couple of teenagers and went to their separate beds. It was pleasurable enough, but it was far from perfect, and it made for impatience and frustration for both of them.

But, if the mills of the gods grind slowly, they grind exceeding sure, and eventually there came word about the annulment. Father Devereux met Dick in the street and stopped to greet him.

'Well, Dick,' he said, 'I believe the date is fixed for the hearing.'

'Yes, Father,' said Dick. 'About six weeks' time.'

'Good.'

'They don't exactly rush themselves.'

'No, but they are a lot quicker than they were,' said Devereux. 'I remember cases taking ten years to come to hearing. And there was one, I believe, in Cork, which took twenty.'

'I've said nothing about this at home, Father.'

'I understand.'

'Mary knows a little, but it's very little,' said Dick. 'I don't want to raise any false hopes.'

'Quite,' said Devereux. 'Naturally, she'll hear nothing from me.'

'If I'm turned down, Father, that's the end of the road, isn't it? There's nowhere else to go, is there?'

'Don't even think of it, Dick,' said the priest. 'Say the prayers . . . and I'll say a few as well.'

Dick wondered how he was expected to pray when he felt the way he did about the whole thing. In truth, he hadn't much hope that the Tribunal, or whatever they called it, would find in his favour.

He said as much to Jack Malone in the pub a couple of nights later. Dick had asked Mary out for a meal, but she couldn't come because she didn't want to leave Auntie Florrie in the house on her own, so he found himself in the pub, drinking brandy and feeling very sorry for himself.

Jack Malone and he were friends of very long standing, going back to their rugby playing days when Jack had been capped for Ireland and Dick had made the Final Trial. Jack was a fine fellow and great company, but his failing was a fondness for the drink, which broke through his resolve at regular intervals and caused him to disappear for long stretches at a time. Because of this weakness his long-suffering wife, Molly, after whom the pub had been named, finally could take it no longer and had left him and gone to England.

At closing time, Jack ushered out the last of the patrons, locked the door, and came back to the bar where Dick was still sitting. Jack poured two brandies for them.

'You're a bit down in yourself,' he said.

'I was over with Mary this afternoon.'

'Did you have a row?'

'No.'

'How's the new house?' asked Jack. 'Great,' said Dick. 'Fits her like a glove. It's a bit ironic, though. I got that house for her with the half-notion that we might share it some day. But I'm afraid the prospect is more remote than ever.'

Jack looked puzzled.

'You have your divorce, haven't you? Is it not recognised?'

'Maybe the State recognises it,' said Dick bitterly. 'But I'm afraid Mary doesn't. I'm trying to get an annulment.'

'Ah,' said Jack.

'You remember the last time Ruth was here?'

'The time we had the rugby match.'

'That's right,' said Dick. 'I started proceedings the day after she left.'

'But that must be two years ago.'

'More,' said Dick. 'It's a long-drawn out process. The Church looks at everything in the light of eternity.'

'What are your chances?' asked Jack.

'Fifty-fifty. Maybe less.'

They both drank in silence a little while.

'It's on the grounds of immaturity,' said Dick.

Jack grinned.

'You? Or Ruth?'

'Both.'

'I suppose that's fair enough. What age was she? Eighteen?'

'Barely. I was twenty . . . and Paul was on the way.'

'Isn't that grounds in itself?'

'No,' said Dick. He had been over it all so many times. 'It's a factor all right. But you'd have to show that undue pressure was exerted on her to get married. It has to be full and free consent.'

'Yeah,' said Jack, thinking of his own marriage.

'But you knew Ruth,' went on Dick. 'Nobody could have forced her to do anything she didn't want to.'

They both contemplated Ruth for a few moments.

'No,' said Dick. 'It's a matter of . . . maturity of judgement. Appreciation of the nature of marriage. All that.'

'In the name of God, how do you prove that?'

'It's not easy,' Dick agreed. 'Luckily Ruth has co-operated. We've had psychological examinations.'

'Holy God!'

'Both of us,' said Dick. 'Her mother's given evidence. And her doctor.'

'What could her mother say?'

'Well,' said Dick, 'it seems the night before the wedding Ruth was in hysterics. Didn't want to go through with it. That sort of thing.'

'And did the mother talk her into it?'

'No, she did that herself,' Dick grinned wryly. 'She couldn't bear to cancel the reception. Send back all the presents.'

Jack nodded, grinning in his turn.

'These are all signs of immaturity,' said Dick. 'And of course, I hardly drew a sober breath all through our engagement.'

'I know, old son,' said Jack. 'I know. Didn't I help you put it all away!'

'The final hearing is next month,' said Dick.

'And what do you think?'

'They don't give any hints . . . but I've a feeling that we haven't enough.'

'I don't know, Dick,' said Jack. 'You're twelve years apart. Ruth's re-married. Why would they want to punish you? I mean, it was Ruth that walked out.'

'Doesn't work that way, Jack,' said Dick, buttoning his overcoat. 'It was either a marriage, or it wasn't.'

They walked to the door.

'I remember that wedding,' said Jack. 'And the weeks leading up to it. The parties.'

'I don't know how we survived.'

'I remember the party at Ruth's house. I think it was the Sunday before.'

'I'm a little vague about that one,' said Dick.

Jack was now launched on a voyage of reminiscence.

'We had a cup match in the afternoon, remember? We beat Bective. You got locked and passed out. Ruth was disgusted with you. I remember people telling her she was going to have a desperate time with you.'

'Well, they weren't wrong,' said Dick, grinning. 'What did she say?'

'She said she didn't care,' said Jack. 'If you put a foot wrong, she could always get a divorce.'

Dick laughed. Jack opened the door.

'Well, goodnight, old son.'

Dick was already out in the street before it dawned on him what Jack had said. He turned back.

'Wait a minute, Jack. Do you remember her exact words?'

'I just told you,' said Jack. "If he puts a foot wrong, I can always get a divorce." That was *it*.'

'Was anyone else there?'

'I dunno.' Jack thought a moment. 'I think Molly was. Yeah, she was. Why?'

'Was she sober?' Dick asked earnestly. 'Ruth, I mean.'

'Course she was. She never touched it in those days. Is it important?'

'I think it could be,' said Dick. 'If that's the way she was thinking, well . . . it's not what you'd call a full commitment.'

He paused a moment, considering it.

'Jack, would you be willing to give evidence?'

'Sure,' said Jack. 'If you think it would —'

'Would Molly?'

'I can't speak for Molly.'

'That's all right, Jack,' said Dick, his mind racing. 'I can ring her. But *you'll* do it?'

'I will, of course.'

Father Devereux answered the urgent ringing at his door. He had been sound asleep and had just a coat thrown over his pyjamas.

'Yes? Who is it?'

'It's me, Father,' said Dick. 'Did I get you up?'

'Who?'

'Dick Moran. I'm sorry it's so late, Father.'

'Is it an accident?'

'No, Father, nothing like that,' said Dick urgently. 'It's about my annulment.'

'Your annulment!' said Father Devereux.

He looked at Dick very strangely.

'Yes, Father. Can I come in?'

Devereux spoke as he might to a child.

'Dick, it's very late. I've a seven o'clock Mass in the morning. Could you come back tomorrow?'

'I've got new evidence, Father. I'd like to put it forward first thing tomorrow.'

'Well, all right, Dick,' said Devereux as patiently as he could. 'We'll do that. Now, why don't you . . .'

'I'd like your opinion on it, Father.' Dick had no intention of being put off. 'It could make all the difference.'

Devereux sighed.

'Oh very well,' he said resignedly. 'I'm awake now anyway.'

He held the door open.

* * * * *

A week later, breathless, but very pleased with himself, Dick Moran caught up with Father Devereux in the street.

'Have you a minute, Father?'

'Yes, Dick?'

'I've just come from Father Clarke,' said Dick. 'They've agreed to hear the new evidence.'

'Well, that's great news, Dick,' said Devereux, genuinely pleased.

'And even better,' said Dick. 'A day has fallen free next Thursday — the only available day for months. They say that if I can have my witnesses in on that day, the date for the final hearing can stand.'

'And that's just three weeks away. Well, Dick, you've been very lucky.'

'Don't I know it!' said Dick. 'But it's vital that I have my witnesses in next Thursday. Jack's OK, of course. And I'm off now to ring Ruth.'

Devereux nodded. Then he put his hand on Dick's arm.

'Just a word of caution, Dick. All this is very encouraging, but I have to warn you against . . .'

'It's all right, Father,' said Dick. 'I know the score.'

'You may be tempted to take some . . . ah . . . close friend into your confidence,' said Devereux seriously, 'but I would strongly advise . . .'

Dick was equally serious.

'I knew all along that it might come to nothing. So that's what I've told Mary. Nothing.'

'I think you're very wise.'

Dick went straight back to his office and rang Ruth. She was very amenable, glad to be rid of him and willing to help him marry somebody else. Of course, she would come to Dublin for the hearing. He could meet the plane and they could have dinner together. She had heard that there was a new French restaurant in Dublin. . . .

Dick grinned into the phone. Trust Ruth. Nothing but the best. And because the hearing could take all day, there would no doubt be lunch as well as dinner, and perhaps even an overnight stay in the swankiest hotel in the city. But he had reached the stage where he would have paid any money to get the annulment finalised.

And there definitely was light at the end of the tunnel, he told Jack when he dropped into the pub to make final arrangements for the trip to Dublin.

Michelle Malone was there, heavily pregnant with Matt's child, his own grandchild. Dick was happy enough about the pregnancy, but unhappy that Michelle refused to marry Matt. She was undoubtedly a young woman with a mind of her own.

Dick said nothing to Mary, beyond telling her that he had some business to attend to in Dublin. She was naturally curious, but didn't press the matter at the time.

However, things took a little longer in Dublin than he had antici-pated. A late dinner with Ruth, her mother, Jack, and Molly Malone, made it undesirable to attempt to drive back to Glenroe that night, so Dick stayed in Dublin and came back the following morning.

And he ran into all sorts of trouble with Mary. It seemed that Michelle had overheard him talking to Jack in the pub and had told Mary he had gone to Dublin with Jack for 'some sort of a get-together'and had mentioned the name of Ruth. It was said in all innocence by Michelle, he later found out, but Mary of course jumped to all the wrong conclusions.

'So why didn't you tell me about your dinner-party?' Mary asked angrily. 'A business dinner, you said!'

'That's right. Personal business.'

'Which went on all night!'

'Mary, I told you,' said Dick. 'I had a few drinks. I didn't want to drive.'

There was a pause.

'I gather you heard that Ruth was there?'

'I heard that you'd gone to see her. And that you'd stayed the night.'

'Not with Ruth, I assure you,' said Dick.

'It doesn't matter anyway,' said Mary coldly. 'Not my business.'

'If it wasn't your business I wouldn't be here talking about it.'

'And if it was my business, why didn't you tell me at the time?'

There was no convincing her, short of telling her the whole story. And he didn't want to do that, not until it had been settled one way or the other, and he could come home either triumphantly or carried on his shield. He remembered that phrase from something he had read in school about the advice given by the Spartan women to their men when they were setting out for war.

Dick was beginning to feel like a Spartan warrior, buffetted about by life in general and by Mary and the Church in particular. No wonder Father Devereux could go about his settled, contented existence. He hadn't an unreasonable woman to contend with. And he didn't have to wait on ecclesiastical tribunals to tell him what his future was to be.

But there *was* light at the end of the tunnel; he kept repeating that to himself. And if Mary had fallen out with him for the time being, she would soon come round when he went to her waving his piece of paper, or whatever it was they gave you when the answer was in the affirmative.

*If* the answer was in the affirmative.

He went through the following few days in a foul humour. And when the time came for him to go to Dublin for the final verdict, he could hardly bring himself to make the journey.

The day before he went, he met Mary in the pub. She was there with Biddy and Miley and would have passed him on her way out with just a cold greeting, had he not put his hand on her arm.

'Oh, Mary,' he said.

'Yes?'

Her manner was still frosty.

'I was wondering if we could meet. . . .'

She hesitated.

'I'm rather busy this week. . . .'

He interrupted her.

'So am I. I was thinking of tomorrow.'

'What day is tomorrow?'

'Wednesday.'

She was still determined to punish him.

'Oh . . . that's a little awkward.'

Dick said urgently, 'It has to be tomorrow. It's important to me.'

She looked at him a moment.

'All right. Tomorrow.'

The following morning he drove to the city. He drove fast and aggressively, snarling at any driver who impeded his progress, blowing his horn at pedestrians and generally behaving in the worst possible way.

When he arrived at his destination, he walked into the room with his shoulders back, his whole demeanour indicating that he didn't give a damn one way or the other. If they wanted to throw him out, well, let them! Nobody was ever going to say that he crawled — or whinged when he lost.

The journey back was much different. He had the car radio blaring as he roared down the dual-carriageway and he grinned happily at the other motorists he passed. He stopped in Bray and bought a large bouquet of flowers and a bottle of wine, plus a new box of cigars for himself.

Thus armed, he arrived at Mary's house at nine o'clock that night. When he handed her the bouquet of flowers, she was pleased, accepting that it was a peace offering, but she gave him no kiss of greeting and merely led him into the sitting room. He waved the bottle of wine and asked her to find two glasses.

It wasn't till the wine had been poured and they were seated on the sofa together that he broached the subject.

'I was in Dublin today.'

'I'm sure that was nice for you.'

'It was.'

The next morning when Miley was arguing with Dinny outside the house, they were interrupted by the sound of a car horn. Dick's car swept up the driveway and in it were Dick and Mary, smiling broadly. Biddy came out to see what the racket was about and she needed only one look at her mother's radiant face to give her the answer.

Soon the news was all over Glenroe and there was a larger attendance at Mass the following Sunday than there had been since

Christmas morning. Mary was surrounded by women anxious to shake her hand, and if there were any unkind remarks to be made about the match they were made in the privacy of the respective homes. Today all was congratulations and well-wishes.

Mary caught Father Devereux after Mass. He was naturally very pleased at the news and, when she asked for a chance to talk to him, he invited Dick and herself over to the presbytery. He put them sitting on the sofa in his sitting room.

'Would you like some tea?'

'Nothing thanks, Father,' said Dick. 'We don't want to hold up your lunch.'

'Right then,' said Devereux. 'Well, first of all, I hope you know how fortunate you've been.'

'I realise that, Father,' said Dick. 'I never *really* felt we'd win.'

'It isn't so much the winning as the speed of it,' said the priest.

Dick couldn't let that go.

'It was twenty-seven months!'

'Sure, that's no time at all, Dick. I know of a case that . . .'

He saw the expression on Dick's face and changed tack rapidly.

'However, that's in the past. We have to look at the future.'

'Exactly,' said Dick.

'Well, first of all, there's the civil side of things. I'm afraid I'm no expert on the law.'

'I'm looking into that now, Father,' said Dick. 'I don't really think it'll be a problem.'

'Good,' said Devereux. 'Then I suppose you're thinking of a wedding sometime in the New Year?'

'The New Year?'

'Or maybe the Spring?'

'Father,' said Dick. 'It's the seventh of May!'

'We were thinking of the summer, Father,' said Mary, putting a restraining hand on Dick's arm.

'Well, that's grand,' said Devereux. 'I didn't think you'd want to wait so long.'

'It's *this* summer we mean,' said Dick.

'But that's out of the question.'

There was a long pause. Dick stared at the priest.

'Why?' asked Mary.

'Didn't they explain to you? About the appeal? The Defender of the Bond . . . that's the Canon Lawyer appointed to oppose the application . . .'

'I know who he is,' said Dick impatiently.

GLENROE – THE BOOK

'He has to appeal the verdict to the Roman Rota.'
The atmosphere in the room became very tense.
'It's a mere formality,' said Devereux consolingly.
Dick was now quite angry.
'And how long is this *formality* going to take?'
'Maybe six months. Maybe more. I'm sorry.'
'Sorry doesn't help!' snarled Dick.
'It's not Father's fault,' said Mary.
'Yes, I know, I know.'
But he didn't feel like forgiving anyone.
'It's only another six months, Dick,' said Devereux.
Mary stood up. She was afraid of what Dick might do.
'I think we should go, Dick. Let Father Devereux have his lunch.'
Dick allowed her to take his arm and lead him to the door. He kept a tight rein on his tongue, because he couldn't trust himself to speak.
However, at the door he turned.
'Do you remember that chap in Greek mythology, Father? The one that rolled the stone up the hill. And every time he reached the top, it rolled back down again and he had to start all over again!'
'Sisyphus?'
'That's the fella. That's me.'

# • CHAPTER SIX •

# GOING TO THE DOGS

ather Tim Devereux leaned across the occasional table and carefully poured a measure of sherry into the two glasses. Then he corked the bottle, sat back, picked up one of the glasses and raised it in a toast to his visitor.

'Well, Paddy,' he said, 'that's great news altogether. Congratulations.'

Paddy Maher picked up the other glass. It felt strange to his fingers, just as the sherry looked foreign to his eye, which was much more accustomed to looking at pints of stout. But he knew what was required of him.

'Thanks, Father,' he said.

He sipped the sherry and tried to give the impression that he was enjoying it.

'A nice drop of oloroso, that,' said Father Devereux.

'Oh aye, aye,' said Paddy. 'Delicious.'

'Well, now, to the business in hand,' said Devereux. 'I don't know what's been holding you back so long from marrying a fine girl like Bernie. I suppose it was the young sister that finally made up your mind for you?'

'They're saying that,' said Paddy. 'But Nuala getting married had nothing to do with it.'

'Now that we're on the subject of Nuala,' said Devereux, 'I want you to tell her to come in and see me. And to bring her young man with her. Do you hear me?'

'Right, Father.'

'Because from what I'm told,' said Devereux severely, 'the only marriage *they* have is from some registry office across the water, and that's no marriage at all.'

'No, Father.'

'I want the two of them in front of me before the altar in double quick time and I'm giving you the job of getting them there. Do you hear me?'

'Right, Father.'

'Right,' said Devereux.

He took another sip of his sherry before continuing.

'Now, about your own plans. Have you made any decisions about a date?'

'We were thinking about Friday week.'

Devereux put down his glass and stared at Paddy.

'You were what?'

'The sixteenth,' Paddy explained.

Devereux permitted himself a broad smile and shook his head.

'I'm afraid, Paddy, I'd want a lot more notice than that.'

'I'm sorry, Father,' said Paddy, 'but that's the best I can do.'

'But sure, God save us, Paddy, there's a million things to be looked after — Birth Certificates, Baptismal Certificates, Letters of Freedom. . . .'

'The two of us were born in the parish,' said Paddy. 'And we never stirred out of it. There shouldn't be any problem at all.'

'Oh now,' said Devereux with an indulgent smile, 'there are always problems. Nothing like this ever works out easy. Why not wait a few more weeks. . . .'

'Has to be Friday week,' said Paddy. 'Didn't you say you wanted to do a rush job on Nuala? Why not us?'

'Nuala's an . . . emergency,' said Devereux.

'So are we, Father,' said Paddy. 'We can't put it off any longer.'

Devereux looked at him a moment. Then he let out a long sigh.

'I see,' he said sadly. 'So that's the way it is. Well, in that case I'll have to see what can be done.'

Paddy stood up and slapped the priest's back.

'Good man, Father! I never doubted you.'

Devereux was startled by the easy familiarity. Paddy was taking this whole thing far too lightly. He felt that a little admonition wouldn't go amiss.

'I'm sorry if I look . . . well . . . shocked, Paddy. But it's a thing I was never used to. And something I can't condone. You understand that. Though I suppose it's common enough these days.'

Paddy looked puzzled.

'However,' said Devereux, 'at least you're doing the decent thing by the girl. Standing by her. I have to admire that.'

He ushered Paddy to the door.

'Bring Bernie in to me this evening and we'll have a chat,' he said.

When Paddy had left, Devereux returned to his unfinished glass of sherry. Young people, he thought. All the old conventions being brushed aside as if they counted for nothing. The world was not at all like the one in which he had been brought up.

He sat back and thought about his own youth in Gougane Barra. Such happy days. Such innocent days. The one love-affair he had ever had, if it could be called a love-affair. Dodie Cronin. He remembered with pleasure her dark hair and laughing face. Even across all the intervening years he could still picture her very clearly. She had been a really lovely, lively girl.

Of course by now she would have changed as much as he himself had changed. She had married his arch-rival for her affections, Maurice Cronin. No doubt by now she had several children — perhaps even grandchildren. He smiled at the thought. Imagine Dodie with grand-children.

No children or grandchildren for himself, however. He had chosen the priesthood. No regrets, of course. He had always intended to be a priest, almost from the day he had made his First Communion. Falling in love with Dodie had been merely an interlude on his way to matu-rity. And life in the Church had been good to him.

Here he was now, curate in a neat little village, well-liked and respected by his flock, who by and large were very decent folk . . . with the odd exception. Here he was, sipping a glass of sherry in the comfort of his own sitting room. Not rich, but then not poor. Able to afford his simple pleasures. The occasional glass such as this. The cherished rack of pipes above the mantelpiece. The occasional trip to Shelbourne Park or Harold's Cross to watch the dog-racing and to place the occasional modest bet.

He picked up again the letter he had received a few days before from his brother, Con. Con, the bookie. An unlikely profession for the brother of a priest . . . or perhaps that should be put the other way around. He read the letter again.

'Dear Tim,' Con had written. 'About that little matter we were discussing last month. I think I've found just the job for us. A neat well-bred bitch that's going to produce great pups in the future, unless I'm totally out of my mind. . . . '

And so on.

The lady in question was at this very moment confined in the small garden at the back of the presbytery. Con was right. Grainne of Glenroe was a fine-looking bitch. A bitch with possibilities. She merely had to be minded and brought to stud at the appropriate time. And no better man than Devereux himself to see to that. He had to admit that he knew a good greyhound when he saw one.

Of course, Con couldn't keep her. Equally certainly she couldn't be kept in the presbytery garden. A place would have to be found for her on one of the surrounding farms, under the care of some sympathetic and competent person. Well, that problem shouldn't be very hard to solve. In fact, he already had just the person in mind.

Father Devereux finished his sherry. He picked up the glass that Paddy had left behind. It was almost full. Very carefully Devereux poured the sherry back into the bottle. Thrift was second nature to him. Not one of the cardinal virtues, perhaps, but one not to be lightly passed over.

There was a discreet knock on his door and Mrs Hefferon came into the room.

'Another visitor for you, Father,' she said apologetically. 'He says it's important.'

'Who is it?'

'Dinny Byrne. I told him you were due up at the church in twenty minutes, but he says he won't keep you.'

'Actually, I'd like to see Dinny, Mrs Hefferon,' said Devereux. 'Send him in.'

While Mrs Hefferon was out of the room, Devereux took from the sideboard the bottle of whiskey he kept for special guests. He set this and a glass on the table.

Mrs Hefferon showed Dinny Byrne in. He was carrying his cap in his hand and he looked a little flustered.

'Thanks, Daisy,' he said to Mrs Hefferon as she left the room. 'Evening, Father.'

'Dinny,' said Devereux. 'Sit yourself down there and I'll pour you a drop of Irish.'

'Fair play to you, Father.'

Dinny sat, but he didn't appear at all comfortable. Something on his mind, thought Devereux, as he poured a generous measure of whiskey.

'Are you not joining me?' asked Dinny.

'I've already had some sherry,' said Devereux. 'Now, what can I do for you?'

Dinny took a quick gulp of whiskey, as if to fortify himself. Then he groped in his pocket and produced a large brown envelope.

'The parish accounts,' he said. 'Young David Brennan asked me to deliver them.'

Devereux took the envelope from him and threw it unopened on the table.

'And you came all this way just to . . .'

'Not exactly, Father,' Dinny interrupted him. 'There was something arising out of the accounts. Something I wanted to mention. Just between the two of us.'

'Oh ho,' said Devereux, because he didn't quite know how to respond to all this seriousness.

'It appears . . . ' Dinny began.

He paused, got up from his seat and went to the door. Daisy Hefferon had left it ajar. Dinny closed it. Devereux watched him in some surprise. This kind of secretive activity was quite unusual for Dinny Byrne. Dinny resumed his seat.

'It appears,' he continued, very formally, 'the accounts are short.' He paused again, as if waiting to see the effect of his words on the priest. Then he announced,

'Four hundred pounds.'

'How much did you say?'

'Four hundred and twenty-nine pounds and a few odd pence,' said Dinny. 'According to David.'

He took another drink, looking at Devereux over the rim of his glass. Devereux laughed.

'Between the two of us, Dinny,' he said, 'I'm the worst book-keeper in the world. In all the years I've been in Glenroe, I've never once got those books to balance, would you believe that?'

There was a moment of silence.

Then Dinny said with great solemnity, 'Four hundred pounds is a lot of money, Father.'

'It is,' Devereux agreed. 'But it'll turn up, never fear.'

He dismissed the subject. 'Now, there's something I want to ask you about, Dinny. . . .'

Dinny held up his hand.

'Father, it's very hard for me to say this. But you're a man who likes a bet.'

Devereux leaned back in his chair and considered this remark.

Dinny ploughed on determinedly.

'And it isn't just what you've often told us . . . just the few bob. Because you see, Father, Biddy and I saw you. Last week. At the dogs. We saw you at the pay-out and you were collecting about four hundred pound. And, well, I said to meself, if a man can win four hundred, he can lose it just as easy.'

He paused.

'Go on,' said Devereux.

'Do you see what I mean, Father?'

Devereux nodded his head soberly, but he felt no anger, just a little sadness.

'You have a very poor opinion of me, Dinny,' he said.

'Indeed I haven't, Father,' Dinny protested. 'But I know a priest is only a man. I only came to say what I know. I said it to nobody else. And it wasn't easy saying it, I can tell you.'

He drained the last of his whiskey. Devereux smiled and poured another small amount into the glass.

'No,' he said. 'I don't suppose it was.'

He stood up.

'I can see I'd better come clean,' he said.

Dinny was on his feet too. 'Now, Father, you've no obligation in the world to tell me anything. . . .'

'Sit down, Dinny, and don't interrupt,' said Devereux. 'Just listen.'

He waited till Dinny had resumed his seat before he continued.

'As you say, I'm fond of a little bet. And I'm in the way of getting information from time to time. You know that too. Well, the source of that information is a brother of mine, who happens to be a bookmaker.'

He gave a slight smile.

'You'll agree that that's a nearly unbeatable combination, Dinny — a priest and a bookie. There are two reasons why Con gives me information. One is that he knows my fifty pence isn't going to ruin the odds; the other is that from time to time he can ask me to oblige him by placing a few bets here and there on his behalf. You understand that if he were seen laying bets himself it would affect the market. They watch people like him. But if a priest is seen laying twenty pounds here and fifty pounds there, nobody pays any attention. You'll hear the odd crack, of course, but that's all.'

'So that money at the dogs . . . ?' said Dinny.

'It wasn't mine, Dinny. Unfortunately. Though I can tell you I stuck the brother for a small contribution to the Youth Club.'

Dinny finished his glass and rose to his feet again.

'I'm sorry if I offended you, Father.'

But Devereux didn't feel offended in the slightest. In fact, he rather admired Dinny for having had the gumption to bring up the subject at all. Most of the parishioners would rather tangle with an alligator than confront a priest.

'The more I think about it, the more I admire you for coming to *me*, rather than discussing it in the pub.'

'It's the last you'll hear of it from me, Father,' said Dinny.

'Oh I'll hear enough of it from the Parish Council, I'm sure.'

'Aye,' said Dinny. 'And now, I know you're in a hurry, so I'll . . .'

'Before you go, Dinny,' said Devereux, 'come out into the back garden and I'll introduce you to a fine little lady friend of mine.'

And so it was that Dinny Byrne came to mind Grainne for Father Devereux. And for co-owner Con Devereux, though *he* never put his nose into the village, but was glad to leave all the responsibility in the hands of his clerical brother.

As he said to Tim,' If you can't trust a priest . . . !'

Now all that had to be done was to keep Grainne fit and well and wait until she came into season.

Mr Dinny Byrne.

'With this ring I thee wed': Biddy looks into the eyes of her new husband.

Another happy couple: Dick Moran and Mary MacDermott.

A happy family snap — Mary, Miley, Denise, Biddy and Dick.

The prices weren't great at the sheep mart.

'George, you'll have nothing to worry about.' 'Yes, Richard.'

Biddy enjoyed Jeff's company at dinner.

Dick, Mary and Denise picking some daffodils for 'Daff Day'.

'Smile for the camera, Denise.'

'Now, blow hard, Denise.'

Dick Moran on a pheasant shoot.

Michelle needed time to think.

Miley and Denise take a stroll.

Stephen and Dinny out for a quiet pint.

In the meantime, Devereux had been musing over the money missing from the Parish Funds. There was something very familiar about the figure of four hundred and twenty-nine pounds. He had seen that amount written down somewhere before.

He went into his study and opened his desk. There were papers everywhere, all in considerable disarray. He hadn't been exaggerating when he had told Dinny that he was the world's worst book-keeper.

He breathed a little prayer to Saint Anthony and went rummaging about. Paper after paper was tossed aside. And then suddenly there it was. He stabbed his finger at it in triumph. The Coal Fund for the poor of the parish! Four hundred and twenty-nine pounds and fifty-eight pence!

He had paid for the coal by cash from the door-to-door collection and the coal merchant had merely receipted the bill. There was no separate receipt. That was why it hadn't got into the accounts with all the other receipts.

At the next meeting of the Parish Council he had great pleasure in producing the piece of paper and waving it in front of David Brennan's nose. Well, he didn't exactly wave it, except in a metaphorical sense, but he savoured the small victory all the same.

Another piece of good news was the discovery that the 'emergency' which Paddy Maher had mentioned had nothing to do with the imminent arrival of a little Maher into the world, but was merely the fact that Paddy and Bernie were emigrating to England and wished to be married before they went.

Devereux felt very contrite for having jumped to the wrong conclusion and, by way of penance, he almost forced himself to apologise to Paddy and Bernie for having misjudged them. On more mature consideration, however, he decided that, as they didn't know what he had been thinking, an unexpected confession might merely upset them needlessly. So he punished himself instead by going a day without a smoke.

Then one morning the phone rang in the presbytery. It was a cheerful Dinny.

'Is that yourself, Father?'

'Dinny,' said Devereux. 'What can I do for you?'

'To tell you the truth,' said Dinny excitedly, 'it's about the oul bitch.'

Devereux was immediately anxious.

'There's nothing wrong with her, is there?'

'Well, now,' said Dinny. 'It's my guess . . . I think she's coming into heat.'

'Are you sure?' said Devereux. 'She's not due to come into season for another two weeks.'

'Try telling that to the congregation of mongrels around the door.'

'Oh?' said Devereux. 'Is that the way of it?'

'The word is out, Father,' said Dinny. 'There's assorted canines from all arts and parts sniffing and clamouring all around the yard.'

'I hope now, Dinny,' said Devereux, being as delicate as possible, 'that no . . . ah . . . .contact has been made?'

'Ah no, Father,' Dinny assured him. 'No, no. I have her securely tied up in her house.'

'Good, good,' said Devereux. 'Now, here's what you'll do. Keep her well locked in, take her food to her, and I'll be around at six o'clock to bring her to the dog.'

'Oh you have that arranged, have you?'

Devereux permitted himself a satisfied little smile into the phone.

'I have indeed. The best stud dog in the county. And remember, I have to bring that lady untainted to the marriage bed. Whatever you do, keep a strict eye on her.'

'Oh rest aisy, Father,' said Dinny.

That evening, promptly at six, Devereux drove up to the Byrne cottage. The place was quiet and there wasn't a dog in sight. Undoubtedly Dinny had been exaggerating about the 'assorted canines'. Miley was standing in the yard talking to George Manning. When they saw him coming they exchanged some quick words.

'Good evening, George. Good evening, Miley,' said Devereux. 'Is your father in?

Miley looked somewhat agitated.

'He is, Father,' he said. 'I mean, he's *not*. He's out with the dog.'

'With the dog?'

'That's right,' said Miley. 'Out for a good long walk.'

'But he was expecting me,' said Devereux.

'Oh yes, he knew you were coming all right,'said Miley. 'But he didn't know you were coming so soon. Like.'

Devereux sometimes wondered if Miley was the full shilling.

'I said six and I'm here at six,' he said. 'This is really very annoying.'

'Oh it is, Father. Sure, I know that well. I tell you what,' said Miley. 'Why don't you go up to the MacDermotts' and wait there.'

'I suppose I might do that,' said Devereux. He just had to make the best of it.

George was standing there with the usual vague, good-natured expression on his face, switching his glance from Miley to the priest and back again, but he made no contribution to the conversation. In fact, he looked rather embarrassed.

'You see,' said Miley. 'Mary was asking for you and she's dying to see you, she said. She told me that only a little while ago.'

This seemed highly unlikely to Devereux, but he didn't argue.

'Yes,' he said. 'That's what I'll do. And the minute Dinny comes, send him across to me.'

As he was turning away he heard the unmistakeable sound of a dog whimpering. He turned back sharply.

'What was that?'

Miley looked at George with something like desperation on his face. He seemed to be silently imploring George to say something.

'Ah,' said George. Then, evidently feeling that that was an inadequate contribution, he added, 'It sounded like a sheep.'

Devereux decided that George wasn't any saner than Miley.

'It's from inside,' he said. 'She's in the house.'

He marched towards the door. Miley kept pace with him, waving his arms about.

'Well, now, isn't that a good one,' he said. 'She must've come back and I never knew it.'

Devereux pushed past him and went into the house. He stopped in surprise at the sight which greeted him.

Dinny was down on his knees, rubbing Grainne of Glenroe with a towel, drying off her wet coat.

There was a basin of water beside him. He had evidently been giving the dog a wash.

'Dinny!' said Devereux. 'What in God's name are you doing?'

Miley muttered something about having to see George and escaped out the door.

'Oh, Father,' said Dinny with exaggerated surprise, 'I didn't see a bit of you there.'

'What are you doing to the dog?'

'I'm just giving her a bit of a tidy-up to have her looking nice and she walking up the aisle.'

Devereux wasn't a bit impressed.

'I'd be very nervous about doing a thing like that to her when she's in the condition she's in,' he said. 'The slightest thing can put them wrong.'

'Ah, divil the fear of her now, Father,' said Dinny. 'I'm telling you. And I put a bit of sheep-dip in the water for good luck.'

'I hope you're right,' said Devereux. 'Let's get her collar on her and I'll be on my way.'

He had an odd sense of things not being quite right. However, Grainne seemed to be in good form, so he took her off to the stud.

It was an expensive business.

'Five hundred pounds,' he told Mrs Hefferon later.

'Glory be to God! Will they be made of gold, or what?' she said.

'Flesh and blood,' Devereux smiled at her. 'Just wait till they start winning races. . . .'

'I hope it keeps fine for you,' said Mrs Hefferon.

But Devereux was quite sure it *would* keep fine for him. A good bitch and a good sire — what more could the quality want! Now he had merely to wait for the happy event.

In time the good news came. Just before Christmas he was met in the street by an excited Dinny.

He shook the priest's hand vigorously.

'She's done it, Father!'

'Do you tell me now?' said Devereux delightedly. 'When did it happen?'

'Last evening,' said Dinny. 'The best litter you're likely to see in a month of Sundays. A grand Christmas present for yourself and the brother.'

'That's great news entirely,' said Devereux. 'I'll have to come out and inspect them.'

'Any time you like,' said Dinny.

But Devereux was so busy during the Christmas week that he didn't get out to see Grainne of Glenroe till Christmas Day.

He had been invited out to the MacDermott home that evening. Despite the death of her husband earlier in the year, Mary MacDermott had decided to host the usual gathering at Christmas. Devereux agreed with her decision. He felt it was right that she should get on with her life. Michael had been an old man, but Mary was still young and attractive, with every prospect of marrying again. Indeed, it was common knowledge in the village that Dick Moran was more than a little interested in helping her to plan a future for herself. Devereux would be happy to go along with that scenario, provided that the position concerning Dick's marriage could be regularised.

He met Dinny outside the church after Mass. Dinny had his brother in tow, Father Jim, the Monsignor. He had come on a visit from America to buy a house for some nuns from his parish who wished to bring a community to Ireland.

'Father,' said Dinny proudly, 'you haven't met me brother. This is Father Devereux, the Curate. And this is Father Jim, the Monsignor.'

Devereux shook hands with the large visitor, making a mental note of the way Dinny had put him in his place on the hierarchical ladder.

'I've heard a lot about you,' he said.

'Father Devereux has a deep interest in greyhounds,' Dinny explained to his brother.

'Oh I wouldn't call it a deep interest,' said Devereux. 'More a pastime.'

'Himself and his brother, the bookie, are the co-owners of the bitch you met in my house the other evening,' said Dinny.

Devereux wished that Dinny would shut up.

Father Jim, the Monsignor, was grinning all over his face.

'Oh yes,' he said. 'With the little pups. Charming.'

Devereux, the Curate, decided to change the subject.

'I hear I may be inheriting a houseful of nuns,' he said.

'It's certainly looking that way,' said Father Jim. 'But don't be too alarmed, Father. They're all sober, house-trained young ladies.'

That evening Devereux made his way out to the MacDermott house. He took Mrs Hefferon with him, because she too had been invited by the thoughtful Mary. During the course of the evening he made a point of nabbing Dinny, who was in earnest conversation with his brother. Father-Jim-the-Monsignor, Devereux remembered, with an unworthy touch of acerbity.

'Excuse me, Father,' he said to the Monsignor. 'Do you mind if I take Dinny away for a few minutes?'

'Please do,' said Father-Jim-the-Monsignor. 'He's giving me a bad time.'

'I have to see these pups,' Devereux explained.

'And I'm coming as well,' said Daisy, appearing at his elbow. 'I want to see these golden wonders!'

'Right, Father,' said Dinny. 'Come on, Daisy.'

He led them across to his own holding and into the outhouse where the happy event had taken place.

It was dark inside, with just a single bulb suspended over the mother and children. Grainne lay on a bedding of straw. Six small pups were climbing all over her and alternately suckling and playing with each other.

Devereux stared at the little creatures. A tiny doubt began to nag at him.

Daisy Hefferon was absolutely delighted.

'Ah the little dotes. Can I pick one up?'

'You better not, Daisy,' said Dinny. 'The mother doesn't like it. What do you think, Father?'

Devereux could manage only a non-committal grunt. He found it difficult to contain his disappointment at the sight of these little runts.

'Come on,' said Dinny. 'We'll leave them alone.'

Outside in the cold evening air, Dinny turned to Devereux.

'Well, Father?'

'Yes, Dinny?' said Devereux, his mind now full of forebodings.

'What do you think of them?' asked Dinny.

'They're very small,' said Devereux.

'Of course they're small,' said Dinny. 'Aren't they only a week old!'

'What I mean is, they're too small,' said Devereux. 'There's something wrong.'

He excused himself and went away. He didn't know what to think. Or rather, he didn't know what he was going to say to Con. Certainly there wasn't a single pup amongst that lot capable of growing into any class of a decent greyhound.

Of course, he had merely had a fleeting glimpse of the litter under a very dim light. Perhaps he was mistaken in his assessment of their merits. He would return in another couple of days and have a second, more detailed, examination. Until then it would be better not to say anything to Con.

But, after all, if there *were* anything wrong with Grainne of Glenroe, it had to be remembered that the bitch had been chosen by Con, not by himself. And he was very glad of this — Con could be very hot-tempered and unreasonable in certain circumstances. Anyone, even the most expert, can be mistaken about a dog. Certainly there could have been nothing amiss with the stud.

But between one thing and another, he didn't get out to see the pups for the next week. On the Friday he dropped into Malone's pub. He knew he'd find Dinny there. And sure enough, there the man himself was, holding up the bar with Stephen Brennan. George Manning was also in attendance.

As Devereux approached them he became aware of a certain furtiveness in their manner. It wasn't anything that he could put his finger on, just a kind of atmosphere which seemed to hang about them. And he thought uneasily that it reminded him of the performance of Miley and George the day he had called to take Grainne to the stud.

However, they all greeted him warmly enough.

'What'll you have to drink, Father?' asked Dinny.

'Ah, nothing, thank you, Dinny.' Devereux found himself being excessively polite and formal. 'I merely want to let you know that I'll be out to see you on Sunday.'

'You're always more than welcome, Father,' said Dinny. 'Is there anything special you want to see me about?'

'The pups, Dinny.'

'Oh aye,' said Dinny, as though he had never heard of them before. 'The pups. Of course. The pups.'

Devereux noticed that Stephen had turned his head away and was making a very careful examination of his finger-nails. He glanced at George, but George's large and frequently expressionless face was even more blank than usual. He turned back to Dinny.

'Will three o'clock be all right?'

'Sure, why wouldn't it,' said Dinny.

'Three o'clock then,' said Devereux.

'On Sunday,' said Dinny.

'That's right,' said Devereux.

He couldn't help adding, with a trace of irony,

'I hope that won't inconvenience you?'

'Inconvenience me?' said Dinny. 'Sure, how could it inconvenience me?'

Devereux made his farewell and left the pub. He had a strong feeling that a very animated conversation started the moment he turned his back, but he put aside the unworthy thought that they were talking about him. After all, he had been wrong in imputing dubious motives to Paddy Maher. He must be getting uncharitable in his old age.

If I'm like this in my forties, he asked himself, what'll I be like when I'm really old?

The next day he spent long hours in the confession-box. It is a job that most priests dislike and he was no exception. He knew it had to be done, and he knew that spiritually, and perhaps even materially, it was very valuable to his flock, but it was hard to remember such things as he listened to the stream of peccadilloes and minor offences and larger miseries which washed over him through the wire mesh.

Finally there came a lull and he wondered hopefully if the flow had dried up for the day. He was just about to gather up his things and leave the box when he heard the door open on the men's side and the scrape of heavy boots on the wooden floor of the confessional, followed by the thump of a pair of solid knees and a muffled groan of pain as the penitent knelt down. Then there was just heavy breathing.

Devereux opened the slide. Through the mesh he caught a glimpse of a familiar grey head, now bowed in prayer. He knew who it was, but the conventions of the situation demanded that he feign ignorance unless the penitent chose to reveal himself.

'Bless me, Father, for I have sinned. . . . '

'How long?' said Devereux.

'Eight months,' said Dinny. He paused in recollection. 'I got drunk four times. . . . '

There was another pause.

'Yes?' said Devereux.

I took the Holy Name maybe once or twice a week. I was late for Mass three times.'

There was another pause.

'Yes,' said Devereux. 'Is there anything else worrying you?'

'Well, there is, Father,' said Dinny. 'I let a man down.'

Father Devereux found himself mentally sitting up and taking notice.

Dinny continued,'I don't know what category that comes under, but . . .'

'Don't mind the category,' said Devereux. 'Was it to do with something serious?'

'Serious enough,' said Dinny.

'Well,' said Devereux. 'Just tell me the story in the simplest way you can.'

'I don't have to name names, do I?' asked Dinny.

'Of course not.'

'Well,' said Dinny. 'The facts are that I was holding a valuable property in trust for this man . . . and I abused me trust.'

'What was the nature of this property?' asked Devereux, though he felt that he already knew the answer.

'It was a greyhound bitch, Father,' said Dinny.

Well, there it was. Devereux sat in silence and waited.

'The bitch in question,' said Dinny, 'came into season on or about the thirteenth of October.'

'The date is of no importance,' said Devereux testily.

'The reason I remember it, Father, is that that was the date she got away.'

Devereux bit his tongue. He couldn't trust himself to speak.

'And in the light of subsequent events,' continued Dinny, 'it's clear that on the same day the thirteenth of October, that self-same bitch committed adultery with a Jack Russell terrier.'

'A Jack Russell terrier!'

Now it all fell into place. When they had been driving home from MacDermott's house on Christmas night, Mrs Hefferon had waxed sentimental over the puppies.

'Aren't they little dotes?' she had said.

'Small.'

'But lovely. Just like my own little Jack Russell.'

What a fool he had been not to have tumbled to it then.

Dinny was still talking.

'How they managed it, I can't tell you, but . . .'

'It's of no importance how they managed it,'said Devereux. 'It isn't the greyhound bitch or the Jack Russell terrier I have here in the confession box. What steps did you take to inform the owner of the bitch of what had . . . ah . . . transpired?'

'None at all.'

'None at all?'

'Sure, I didn't know, Father,' said Dinny, 'until after the pups were born.'

'I see,' said Devereux. He saw only too clearly. 'And when you *did* find out, did you go and tell him then?'

'That's the very advice I came to you for, Father,' said Dinny.

Devereux was silent for several moments. He wanted to collect his thoughts. He also wanted to control himself.

He said finally, 'Normally, I'd require you to go and see this man and lay the whole sorry story before him. But, in the circumstances, there would seem to be no point in that.'

'Whatever you say, Father,' said Dinny. 'But could you tell me . . . you see, I'm not well-up in these things . . . But would it be true that under the seal of the confessional, you yourself wouldn't be able to discuss this matter with me if we were to meet outside?'

'I believe that would be the case,' said Devereux in very measured tones.

'Or with anybody else?' asked Dinny.

'Naturally.'

'Like for instance,' continued Dinny, 'this man that I let down has a brother, a bookmaker, who's the co-owner of the bitch. Could I take it that . . . ?'

Devereux found his voice rising slightly.

'I think you know very well,' he said, 'that in all these matters I would be utterly and unconditionally bound.'

'I understand, Father,' said Dinny.

Devereux breathed heavily a moment.

'Have you more to tell me?' he said at last.'Not a thing that I can put me mind to at this minute.'

'Very well,' said Devereux. 'For your penance you'll say the Rosary.'

'Do you mean a decade, Father?'

'The full Rosary,' said Devereux, at last achieving a measure of satisfaction. 'The Sorrowful Mysteries.'

When Dinny had left the box, Devereux sat for some time contemplating the vicissitudes of life. He was also wondering just how he was going to explain all this to his brother.

Finally he rose. The church was empty as he walked through it, save for one lone penitent at the back who was telling his beads. The priest went into the vestry and put his things away. Then he locked the vestry door behind him and came out into the frosty evening. A dark figure was standing on the steps of the church.

'Dinny?'

Dinny came across to the priest.

'Good evening, Father,' said Dinny cordially. 'That's a hardy one.'

'It certainly is,' said Devereux. 'Did you have a good Christmas?'

'Very quiet, Father. And yourself?'

'Oh very peaceful, thank God,' said Devereux.

They began to walk towards the gates of the church.

'On the matter of the pups, Dinny . . . '

'The pups?'

Devereux said carefully, 'I wouldn't want to see any of them put down, if that could be avoided. Do you think you'll be able to find homes for them?'

'I'll do me best, Father,' said Dinny.

'Good man,' said Devereux. 'There must be someone who wants a short-legged greyhound. Or a very speedy Jack Russell.'

'Aye,' said Dinny.

They paused at the gates.

'Well,' said Devereux, 'I suppose we had better get in out of the cold.'

'A drop of hot punch is called for, Father.'

Devereux hesitated a moment.

'Before I leave you, Dinny,' he said, 'could I just say that in the course of a career that's been admittedly fairly sheltered . . . I've never met a more devious man than yourself.'

Dinny didn't smile.

'Thank you, Father,' he said. 'A man can only do his best.'

'You'd have made a great Jesuit.'

As Devereux walked away he heard Dinny calling from behind him.

'A Happy New Year to you, Father.'

Without turning, Devereux replied,

'And the same to you, Dinny.'

# · CHAPTER SEVEN ·

# THE BIG HOUSE

When Biddy MacDermott and Miley Byrne announced their engagement, George Manning felt a certain frisson of satisfaction go through his large frame. After all, Miley had come to *him* for advice on the best way to approach the delicate subject of a marriage proposal and George had provided what he had considered to be an excellent recipe for success.

And his confidence had not been misplaced. Miley had succeeded in his quest for Biddy's hand.

Miley came to him the next day.

'Fair play to you, George,' he said. 'You put the right words into me mouth.'

'It was nothing, Myles,' said George modestly. 'I feel sure that you would have succeeded with Biddy no matter what words you used.'

'Ah well, now,' said Miley, 'I just want you to know that I appreciate what you did. And Biddy appreciates it too.'

'Good lord,' said George. 'You surely didn't tell her you took advice from me!'

'Ah no, I didn't do that exactly,' said Miley. 'But she would appreciate it if she knew, like.'

And he insisted on buying George a drink.

George was glad that he had been of use. He often worried about his position in the little village of Glenroe. Even though his family had been there longer than most of the other residents, he sometimes felt that people didn't really accept him as one of themselves. They looked at the Big House in which he lived and the two hundred acres that went with it. They listened to his accent and took note of the eccentric profession he followed, that of naturalist and illustrator of books on nature. They treated him with courtesy and a few surreptitious smiles behind his back. But he felt that they didn't accept him as one of their own.

'They think I'm English,' he said to Miley in one of his rare confidential moments.

'Ah no,' said Miley.

'Oh they do,' said George. 'My accent you see.'

'Ah,' said Miley profoundly.

109

'Just because I went to a Public School and have a brother-in-law who sits in the House of Lords doesn't make me an Englishman, you know.'

'Sure, I know that,' said Miley. 'I know that well.'

'Or a member of the aristocracy,' said George. 'As a matter of fact, most members of the aristocracy wouldn't wish to be seen in the same room with me.'

Miley looked his disbelief, but kept his mouth shut.

'I'm as Irish as you are, Myles,' said George.

There was a long moment of silence before Miley replied.

'Sure, of course you are,' he said. 'What are you having?'

'A pint of bitter,' said George. 'And another thing, they think I'm rich.'

'Ah well, now, that's one thing they don't think,' said Miley.

'Oh they do.'

'Not at all,' said Miley. 'Sure, everybody knows you haven't got a shilling.'

'Oh,' said George.

He digested the remark. He wasn't at all sure that he welcomed this confident assertion that everyone in the village knew the intimate and rather gruesome details of his financial position. It was one thing for him to say it, but quite another to have it confirmed so definitely.

On the other hand, it *was* true that he didn't have a shilling. Well, not *literally* true, of course. But at the moment he had no commissions and his sort of work demanded commissioning. It wasn't the kind of thing one could dash off in a hurry and hope to dispose of in the commercial market. It necessitated a large investment of time and travel and patient observation, often over a year or two. It needed a committed publisher who was prepared to undertake the necessary financial outlay and to wait a considerable time for any return. And just at the moment no such publisher was to be seen on the horizon.

Sloe Hill was a fine house and had been in the Manning family for hundreds of years. It was also very large and really too much for a single man. It swallowed money in maintenance and repairs. It echoed hollowly to his footsteps as he wandered around its many rooms.

Of the two hundred acres attached to the house, about a hundred were rented out for tillage. A large portion of the remainder was woodland, ideal for the observation of flora and fauna, but hardly a source of great financial revenue. Apart from his work, when he got it, George had very little income. His father had invested his money in the Far East: rubber plantations in Malaya, tin mines in Indonesia, that sort of thing. It had no doubt seemed a good idea at the time, but the course of political and economic history had changed all that and

George's inheritance was a meagre one indeed, hardly enough to keep the carnivorous Canis Lupus confined to the hall, let alone to drive him away from the front door.

All in all, he had to admit to himself that the prospect was dismal. And it was in this frame of mind that he approached young Paul Moran in his capacity as a solicitor to ask him to put his toe into the water, as it were, to test the possible reactions to the notion that Sloe Hill might conceivably come onto the market should he, George, at some unspecified date in the future, which might never come to pass, all things considered, decide to sell. Nothing more than that, all strictly confidential.

Which is why he was so annoyed when Dick Moran called out to Sloe Hill the next day and indicated that he would be a prospective bidder should the house come up for auction.

George considered Dick to be something of a Canis Lupus himself, a friendly enough man on the surface and no doubt possessed of many sterling qualities invisible to the naked eye (George was nothing if not charitable in his judgements) but a man who seemed constantly to be devoted to the task of feathering his own nest. Not that such activity was entirely reprehensible in a businessman, provided it was practised in moderation, though George personally looked on the pursuit of financial gain as rather infra dig.

He was also congenitally incapable of indulging in the pursuit himself.

As usual, George was very polite to Dick when he came to call and offered him the last drink from the last bottle of sherry, the last bottle of *anything*, apart from tomato ketchup, left in the house.

However, he quickly disabused him of the notion that Sloe Hill was up for sale.

'Where did you hear that?' he asked.

'On the grapevine,' said Dick.

'I've given no such instructions,' George said. It was a pale sort of fib, which he felt was justified by the breach of confidence.

He climbed up the ladder again and resumed the job of fixing the Christmas decorations, which Dick's arrival had interrupted.

'The house was always full at Christmas,' said George, more to himself than to Dick. 'Or perhaps it just seems that way, looking back. A trick of hindsight no doubt.'

'No, you're probably right,' said Dick. 'Christmas used to be a time for staying home. Not any more.'

'I remember one year we were snowed in,' said George. 'Seven of us playing a game of Monopoly. It went on for six days.'

He came down the ladder again and faced Dick.

'The upkeep is appalling now, of course. I should hate to have to sell, but . . .'

'You may have to?'

'Yes,' said George. 'If all else fails. I'm not the most provident person in the world. But the house is not up for sale at the moment.'

As soon as he had got rid of his visitor, he quickly made his way back to Paul to take his business out of that young man's hands and restore it to the venerable firm of solicitors in Merrion Square who had been handling the Manning affairs for one hundred and eighty years.

He was torn with remorse at the prospect of selling the family home and he disliked the idea that Dick Moran might buy it. Not that George was a snob — such an unworthy outlook would have been abhorrent to him — but he felt that there was a certain order innate in the universe, a certain sense of the fitness of things, which demanded that a house like Sloe Hill should be owned only by someone who was capable of appreciating it. He didn't think that Dick Moran had that capacity, with all due respect to his other, invisible, sterling qualities.

Furthermore, there was the question of Mary MacDermott.

George was very fond of Mary. Whenever he had to introduce her to a stranger he always did so as 'my most important neighbour'. He had long admired her, but, of course, while her husband was alive, the idea of making any advances had been totally unthinkable. Now that she was a widow, things were rather different, though time must be allowed to elapse in conformity with the normal decencies.

Dick Moran, however, was showing no such scruples and was pressing his suit with all the high-powered efficiency of a rotary iron in a dry-cleaning establishment. And George had the feeling that Dick's desire to purchase Sloe Hill wasn't altogether divorced from his evident designs upon Mary MacDermott.

To see Mary ensconced in the house would be extremely pleasurable; to see her ensconced there in the company of Dick Moran would be rather like rubbing salt in the wound while the knife was still present.

However, the Fates smiled upon George. On the very day that the auction was taking place, a phone call brought him a lucrative commission in the West of Ireland. He dashed back from taking the call in Glenroe (his own phone was out of order for reasons which were too painful to mention) just in time to halt the bidding between Dick Moran and Dinny Byrne's brother, the Monsignor from America, who was interested in buying the house for a community of nuns. They had reached the substantial figure of three hundred and thirty

THE BIG HOUSE

thousand pounds, but George hadn't the slightest hesitation in turning his back on such a sum. Certain things were beyond price.

'I say,' he called out to the auctioneer, who was in full flight.

'Yes, Mr Manning?' said the auctioneer. 'I'm afraid we had to start without you.'

'That's perfectly all right,' said George. 'I take it the auction is still in progress?'

'Going rather well, actually.'

'Good,' said George. 'You see, I'm afraid it's all off.'

'Off?'

'I'm not selling,' George explained. 'I hope it hasn't been too inconvenient.'

He looked at the surprised people who were gathered round the steps of Sloe Hill.

'It's been awfully good of you to come,' said George politely. 'It's been lovely seeing you and . . . ah . . . Good afternoon.'

There was a mixture of shock and delight on the faces of the crowd. The auctioneer was visibly annoyed. He gathered up his papers and left in a state of considerably elevated dudgeon.

'George, we're delighted,' said Mary.

'Did you come into money?' asked Biddy.

'Biddy, don't be rude!' said Mary.

But George didn't mind. He told them about his commission. Miley slapped him on the back.

'Good man yourself,' he beamed.

Dick wasn't so happy. But he was a pragmatic man and knew how to accept the inevitable.

'You had us all going there,' he said to George. 'You were headed for a great price.'

George was so pleased with the way things had turned out that he looked kindly on even Dick Moran.

'Actually, I have rather a good idea,' he said. 'You know I have a hundred and twenty acres under the plough? Well, I *do* still need a rather large injection of cash, so I thought, why not hold onto the woods and gardens and sell the tillage. What do you think of that?'

'You mean, you'd like *me* to sell it?' said a surprised Dick.

'Well, naturally, Richard,' said George. 'You're the local man.'

He went off to work in the West of Ireland in a happy frame of mind. And it was a couple of months before he arrived back in Glenroe again.

The first news he heard was the disturbing account of Mary MacDermott's ordeal at the hands of a few villains who had broken

113

into her house one night. Happily, it had all ended well with the apprehension of the desperadoes and Mary herself had not been injured.

George went out to see her immediately. He found her unexpectedly forgiving, after her experience.

His heart swelled towards her. He drank the coffee she had poured for him with the reverence due to a libation from the gods.

There was a little pause in the conversation.

'Now, George,' said Mary. 'Did you want anything in particular?'

'Yes, indeed,' said George. 'I want to ask you a great favour.'

'Yes?'

'You see,' said George, 'my publisher has come over from London and he wants to bring all his Irish authors out to dinner. Well, of course I said yes. One must show the flag at these things.'

'Of course,' said Mary.

'And of course it's likely to be a fairly decent dinner,' said George. 'The problem is that chaps are expected to bring wives, loved ones, that kind of thing. Well, wives *or* loved ones. Not both, I imagine. But since I don't have either, I was wondering if you would do me the honour . . .?

'Of course I will,' said Mary. 'When is it?'

'Tomorrow evening,' said George.

'Oh,' said Mary.

'You'll find them a most interesting group,' said George. 'All naturalists, of course. They're rather hoping that Quincey will turn up.'

'Quincey?' said Mary.

'The greatest living authority on the click beetle,' said George.

But Mary couldn't make it on the night in question. She was most apologetic, but she had promised Aunty Florrie that she would go out to see her. George quite understood. It was entirely his own fault for not asking her sooner.

He hid his disappointment and went away.

On the morning after the dinner George called into the Moran office in Glenroe. He was just in time to meet Matt Moran coming out.

'You're not looking for me, are you?' asked Matt.

'No,' said George. 'I *did* hope to find your father.'

'You won't get him here,' said Matt. 'Not on a Saturday.'

'Oh is it Saturday?' said George. 'How very annoying.'

'Can I help?'

'Well, I have some papers here he is anxious to see,' said George. 'Do you think he's at home?'

'Sure to be,' said Matt. 'Can I give you a lift?'

'I'll walk up, thank you very much,' said George. 'It's a beautiful morning.'

He waved goodbye to Matt and set off at a brisk walk.

It really was a lovely morning. George thought that surely the Deity was in his heaven and everything was absolutely spiffing with the world. He smiled at the Sugarloaf, nodded to cows in fields and positively beamed at the milkman when the float passed him on its way up the steep incline. He even ventured a bar or two of a song.

Dick Moran's house stood shining in the sunlight on the top of its little hill. The milk float passed him again, this time descending. George waved a second cheery greeting and strode up to the door.

Just as he raised his hand to ring the bell, the door was opened. George paused in mid-movement, his hand frozen.

Before him stood Mary MacDermott, clad only in a dressing gown. They stared open-mouthed at each other.

A most embarrassing moment, the sort of thing that remains with one for quite a long time afterwards.

He thrust the papers into her startled hand and fled.

Most embarrassing. And really quite distressing. It quite took the sunshine out of the morning.

Time was a great healer. And the flora and fauna undoubtedly helped. He immersed himself in work in the Burren and when he finally emerged again and found that Mary MacDermott was in fact going to marry Dick Moran, the whole affair had lost its sting. He was able to meet her and work with her, when she came over to Sloe Hill to help with the deer, without any tremors of unrequited love agitating his large frame.

In fact, he was really rather pleased with himself at the way he had withstood the slings and arrows etc. It showed that there was good stuff in the Manning strain.

Of course, Mary didn't help all that much with the deer. The plain fact of the matter was that Dick Moran became jealous of the time she was spending in Sloe Hill and inevitably she withdrew her services. However, George managed to find a suitable substitute in his sister's daughter, the Hon. Fiona March, who came across from England to stay with him. A high-spirited young lady, very pretty, she was quite a good scout underneath it all. She came, George imagined, as much to get away from the attentions of her mother, George's sister, Antonia, as to help her uncle. Antonia was rather overbearing, not the sort of person one would like to spend one's time with on a desert island, and no doubt her daughter found her very oppressive.

He liked having Fiona about the place. She brought youth and vitality with her, even if George found himself having to exercise a certain amount of in loco parentis when she showed a decided penchant for collecting unsuitable young male companions.

In the spring the news came of the death of Paddy Maher, in a road accident in England. Bernie, his handsome young widow, returned to Glenroe with money in her purse, looking for a business to invest in. She went straight to George and proposed to him the idea of turning Sloe Hill into a Guest House. She was willing to invest her insurance money and her own considerable expertise in the project.

After some initial misgivings, George became quite enthusiastic at the prospect of having the house full of people again. But there were complications. When George innocently suggested to Bernie that she should come and live in Sloe Hill with him, she thought he was proposing marriage. And when later he tried to explain that he hadn't meant marriage at all, she thought he was proposing living in sin and she slapped his face.

It was all very bewildering . . . and they hadn't even one guest in the place yet.

George had bought himself a new lens for his camera and, after the stormy scene with Bernie, he set off for Avoca to try the thing out. Little did he realise that the Fates were about to poke their noses into his affairs again.

He was photographing frogs when he met Shirley Rosenbloom. She was standing on the river bank looking down at the water.

'Don't move,' George warned her. 'Stay exactly as you are.'

She nodded, arranged the jacket of her suit, patted her hair and smiled for the camera. But George was interested only in the frogs and walked past her down to the water's edge.

'Thank you so much,' he said, when he had taken his picture. 'I was most anxious not to disturb them.'

'Disturb what?'

'The frogs,' he explained. 'They were mating. Of course, frogs generally are.'

'Are they?'

'Yes, I'm afraid so. Night and day. They're at it all summer. Some of them actually grow little horny tubercles on their arms to prevent them . . . ah . . . falling off.'

'I never knew that,' said Shirley.

George was now taking note of this attractive young lady standing before him. She was disturbingly pretty, he observed, even if she was obviously a colonial and barely came up to his chest.

'Forgive me for asking, but are you American?'

'Yes, I am.'

'Well, you've been awfully helpful,' said George. 'Would you like some coffee?'

'Yes, I would,' she smiled at him.

'Good,' said George. 'Come along then.'

In the bar they exchanged names. Shirley, he learned, despite her Jewish name, had an Irish grandmother who had taught her the Moore Melodies, and she was tickled pink, or whatever the phrase was, to find herself actually looking at the Meeting of the Waters. George found her quite jolly and volunteered to take her to see the church where Percy French had been married.

'The Mountains of Mourne,' said Shirley.

'Another of Granny's favourites, I take it?'

'Yeah.'

She had rented a car and was looking for some place to stay for one or two nights. George racked his brains for suitable accommodation before it suddenly dawned on him.

'I say! I've got a place. In fact I own one. I'd forgotten.'

'How could you possibly forget owning a guest-house?'

'Well, you see,' George explained, 'I haven't owned it for long.'

'You mean you just bought it?'

'No,' said George. 'I've had it for about three hundred years. My family, that is.'

Shirley looked at him.

'George,' she said, 'you are a most confusing person. Are you really Irish?'

'Of course I am.'

'You don't sound Irish,' said Shirley.

George was indignant.

'I would say I sound at least as Irish as your friend Thomas Moore did!'

But out of deference to her preconceptions he threw a few begorrahs and bejapers into the conversation.

They got along famously together and that evening he brought her back to Sloe Hill. The house, the woods and the deer enchanted her.

'Is it really three hundred years old?'

'The original house was,' said George. 'This one is actually quite new. About 1840.'

'Where I come from,' said Shirley, 'an 1840 house is a National Monument!'

Fiona had gone to England for a short stay and so Sloe Hill was empty. George offered to transfer himself to the Gate Lodge, in order to observe the proprieties, but Shirley said that it would be too scary on her own in the big house.

Bernie arrived in the following morning and was cooking breakfast in the kitchen when George came down the stairs singing loudly. He was dressed in pyjamas and dressing gown. He was surprised to see Bernie and greeted her rather warily.

'Good morning, George,' said Bernie. 'I was just going to call you.'

George looked at the table, which was laid for two.

'I'd say you're surprised to see me,' said Bernie. 'I'm sorry about yesterday.'

'Quite all right,' said George, but he kept a safe distance between them, just in case.

'I was wrong, I know that now,' said Bernie. 'I was always like that — going off the deep end. And it's just stupid to live out. I'm moving in, from today.'

'Ah,' said George, without any great conviction. 'Wonderful.'

Just at that moment, Shirley entered the kitchen. She was wearing a frilly nightie.

'Hi, George,' she said.

George resigned himself to the inevitable.

Bernie emerged from behind the door of the fridge and stared at Shirley.

'Hi,' said Shirley to her.

'Bernie,' said George, 'I'd like you to meet Miss Rosenbloom. She's our first guest. And this is our Manageress, Bernie Maher.'

He steeled himself for what was coming. Bernie gathered up her things, walked over to George and slapped him across the face. Then she turned to Shirley.

'I'm not blaming you,' she said. 'You're just another victim.'

And she walked out, banging the door behind her.

'Ah,' said George.

'I'm really sorry, George,' said Shirley.

'Whatever for?'

'Well, she was obviously close to you. . . .'

'Good lord, no,' George protested. 'She's my business partner, nothing more. I'm not awfully sure how to explain this, but I feel I should. After all, this is your first night in Ireland. . . .'

'It's been very exciting,' said Shirley, looking up at him.

'Where shall I start?' said George. 'I'm afraid it's all rather . . . labyrinthine. . . .'

By the time they had finished their eggs, sausages and bacon, everything had been explained, evidently to Shirley's satisfaction. She's such an uncomplicated person, George thought. She faces up to things without resorting to feminine hysteria or other female aberrations.

Shirley had reckoned on staying two or three nights, but, in the event, she stayed for six. However, inevitably the day came when she packed her bags. George was a little sulky as he carried them out to her car.

'I can't see why you have to rush off,' he said.

'Who's rushing off?' said Shirley. 'I've been here a week.'

'No, you haven't.'

'Well, six nights.'

George put on his most petulant face.

'I thought you liked it here,' he said.

'I love it,' said Shirley. 'And you've been terrific, showing me everything. But I still have to see County Kerry and County Clare and County Connemara and . . .'

'Connemara is not a county,' said George.

'Well, I have to see it,' said Shirley. 'And I've only got a week left.'

Before she could leave, Mary MacDermott drove up. Shirley ran back into the house, telling George that she had already met one of his lady friends — and one was enough, thank you very much.

Mary had come to invite Bernie and George over to dinner.

'Well,' said George. 'I rather fancy that Bernie won't come. You see, she keeps hitting me.'

The upshot of the matter was that he prevailed on Shirley to remain another night and accompany him to the dinner. And it was a most pleasant evening. Shirley fitted in as if she had known these people all her life and, when George became aware that Mary was looking at the two of them in a sort of knowing fashion, he didn't mind one little bit.

When they arrived back in Sloe Hill that night, George felt happier than he had ever felt before. They stood in the hall together while Shirley admired the peacock wallpaper.

'Original William Morris,' said George.

Both of them were unwilling to have the evening end.

Finally George said,

'Shall we have a nightcap?'

'I'd love one,' said Shirley.

George was making his way into the drawing room, when she placed her hand on his arm.

'I've got some brandy in my room,' said Shirley.
'Ah,' said George.
'Let's go up,' said Shirley.
George Manning looked into the eyes of Shirley Rosenbloom.
'Why not.'

## · CHAPTER EIGHT ·

# FOR WORSE OR BETTER

'Three weeks this Saturday,' said Dinny Byrne.
He was standing with a mug of tea in his hand, watching his son, Miley, filling the sprayer and attaching it to the tractor.

'What?' said Miley absently.

'The wedding,' said Dinny.

'Oh aye.'

'Is it not near time you were making the arrangements?'

Miley looked up at him.

'What arrangements? Sure, isn't the church booked?'

'What about the invitations?'

'They're all gone out.'

Dinny took the mug of tea from his lips.

'They're what?'

'Last week,' said Miley. 'Did I not tell you?'

Dinny was very offended.

'You did not! You didn't consult me ayther. And I giving you away.'

'Well, it'll be the first thing you *ever* gave away. What did you want to be consulted about?' Miley was genuinely surprised.

'I want to know who's being asked,' said Dinny. 'Matter of courtesy.'

'Begod,' said Miley, 'I couldn't tell you who was asked and who wasn't. I let Biddy and the Mammy get on with it.'

Biddy MacDermott arrived on the scene. She was stamping along with her hands deep in the pockets of her duffel coat. She came straight to Miley. He could see immediately that she was not in good humour.

'What about the spuds?' she asked, by way of greeting.

'What about them?' said Miley.

'You were to start burning them off.'

'I know. I'm doing it.'

'You were to do it yesterday.'

'Well, I'm doing it now,' said Miley sharply. 'Do you not see me?'

Biddy looked coldly at him a moment. Then she turned to Dinny.

'Don't be starting on *me* now!' said Dinny before she could speak. 'What's wrong with *you*?'

Dinny turned his head away and stared across the yard, injured dignity showing in every movement.

'He's annoyed about the invitations,' said Miley.

'We didn't bother to post yours, Dinny,' said Biddy. 'I have it for you above in the house.'

'It's not his own one he's annoyed about,' said Miley.

'I'm able to talk for meself, you know,' said Dinny. He turned to Biddy. 'I suppose you consulted your mother about the invitations?'

'Of course we did.'

'And why wouldn't you!' said Dinny.

He started to walk back to the cottage.

'I suppose we *should* have asked you,' said Biddy contritely. 'I'm sorry.'

'Begod, miss, so you should be.'

'Will you come up later and we'll go over the list? And then if there's anyone you want to ask we can add the names.'

'It's a bit late in the day,' said Dinny, a bit mollified, but milking the last drop.

'I don't know what more we can do,' said Biddy. 'Come up in half an hour.'

'Fair enough.'

Biddy turned back to Miley.

'I'm going down to the tunnel. Don't forget the spuds.'

'I'm doing it, I'm doing it!'

Biddy walked off down the hill.

'She can be very aggravating, do you know that!' Miley said to his father.

They stood a moment in silent understanding.

'It's the way with women,' said Dinny. 'They're better with aggravations than they are with invitations.'

Later on Mary MacDermott showed Dinny and Miley the list of invitations. She started with the names from her own side. There were a lot of them.

'And the last name you know well enough,' she said as she finished reading. 'Auntie Florrie.'

'Aye,' said Dinny.

'And that's it,' said Mary. 'You won't know many of them, but you'll meet them on the day. They're not too bad.'

Dinny said, 'There doesn't seem to be anyone from our side.'

'Oh that was just *our* list,' said Mary. 'Here's yours.'

She handed him a another sheet of paper. He studied it a moment.

'How many was on your list, Mary?'

Mary felt a little uncomfortable.

'Fifty-eight.'

'And we have five,' said Dinny. 'And one of them is meself.' He added, heavily, ' I suppose I should be grateful you're inviting *me*.'

He looked again at the list.

'Mr and Mrs Pat Barry. *They* won't come — they're in Canada. Father Jim. We won't see *him*. And that leaves . . . Peter Donovan.'

Miley smiled at Mary.

'Me Uncle Peter.'

'And with the help of God,' said Dinny, 'he won't come ayther.'

'He's your wife's brother, Dinny,' said Mary.

'Aye,' said Dinny, dismissing Uncle Peter, 'and we haven't heard from him for ten years.'

'Travels the oceans of the world,' said Miley.

'Aye,' said Dinny. 'And the further he travels the better.'

He returned to the list.

'Now let me see.'

However, when he was put to it, Dinny couldn't think of anyone else he wanted to invite, apart from the O'Briens from Slievebracken. But honour had been satisfied.

'If I think of any more, I'll let you know,' he told Mary.

'Fine,' said Mary. 'Now, can I offer you a drink before you go?'

Miley stood up before Dinny could reply.

'He doesn't want a drink at all,' he said. 'Sure, isn't Carol only home from Egypt and you haven't had a chance to talk to her.'

As Dinny and Miley walked back to the cottage, they saw Matt Moran's car reversing out of the yard and driving away. Matt waved to them as he went by, but he didn't stop.

'Isn't that most peculiar now,' said Miley.

'Maybe he left something for us.' said Dinny.

'But isn't it a wonder he wouldn't stop?'

Dinny led the way in through the door. He came to a sudden halt.

'Holy God!' said Dinny.

A little man stood in the kitchen, a smiling little man in a long black coat, whose face glowed with the innocence of a small child.

'Dinny Byrne,' he said gently.

Miley had now come in. He brushed past his father, a delighted expression on his face.

'Peter! Will you leave it there!'

He shook Peter's hand enthusiastically

Dinny's enthusiasm was considerably less than his son's.

'Where in the name of God did *you* come from?'

'I'm here for the wedding,' said Peter mildly. He took his invitation from his pocket.

'Well, begod, isn't that great news altogether,' said Miley.

'The wedding's not for three and a half weeks,' said Dinny coldly.

'Ah well', said Peter, 'I like to be early for these things.'

'And what do you intend doing for the next three and a half weeks?'

'Oh I'm as free as the air,' said Peter pleasantly. 'I came home last week from a cruise to the Carribean and the ship's having a refit, so I've a month.'

'A month?!?'

'I'll need some place to sling my hammock,' said Peter, beaming at the two of them.

Peter had spent his life as a steward on cruise liners and he liked to interject the occasional nautical expression into the conversation. He had sailed on the Queen Elizabeth, the Mauretania and almost any other large ship you cared to mention.

'There was one ship he never sailed on and I was always sorry,' Dinny said to Mary later on.

'What was that?'

'The Titanic!'

But despite Dinny's best efforts to head him off by protesting that there was no bed to spare, Peter soon had himself ensconced in the cottage. He achieved this by charming Mary MacDermott, as he charmed every woman he met, and she discovered that she had a spare divan bed, which she insisted on lending to Dinny for his guest.

Miley was quite happy to have his uncle home, despite Dinny's dislike of the returned sailor. But there were other troubles on his mind. For one thing, Biddy had got very touchy of late. She took the nose off him time and time again. There seemed to be no pleasing her.

And Matt Moran was certainly no help at all in soothing the nerves of a worried man.

'Oh by the way, Miley,' he said when they were having a drink together, 'I got the invitation. Thanks.'

They both sat in silence for a moment.

'Isn't it funny?' said Matt thoughtfully.

'What?'

'How quickly these things creep up on you.'

Miley gave a sigh.

'It surely is.'

Matt grinned at him and slapped him on the back.

'Only three weeks of freedom left.'

Miley tried to match his smile, but his mouth refused to obey him.

Mary told him that it was only natural to get edgy at a time like this.

'You find you're a bit short with each other,'she said reassuringly. 'But it's very usual. You start to get doubts. . . .'

Miley interrupted her quickly.

'Oh there's no question of that in the wide world. Ah no.'

But he couldn't look her straight in the eye.

For her own part, Biddy wasn't finding it easy to come to terms with the approaching event. She had difficulty in sleeping and often got up before cockcrow to go out and do some work which might well have been left till later.

Early one morning Carol found Biddy working in the garden.

'Do you know what time it is?' asked Carol, who was huddled into a warm dressing-gown against the cold.

'No.'

'Seven o'clock. What are you doing out here?'

'I didn't sleep very well,' said Biddy.

Carol smiled.

'Are you getting worried?'

'No,' said Biddy, with more vehemence than conviction. 'I was just cold. I lent Dinny a pair of blankets for Uncle Peter and then I couldn't find the spare ones.'

'They're in the chest in Mam's room,' said Carol. 'But you don't have to worry. In a couple of weeks you'll have Miley to keep you warm.'

She went laughing into the house.

Biddy dug her trowel savagely into the ground. Things were going to be very . . . *different* . . . when they were married. She hadn't quite realised *how* different. And in precisely what way.

She redoubled her attack on the soil and tried to put the thought away from her.

A few days later Miley came across her in the workshed. She was throwing plastic containers about in a rather over-vigorous fashion.

'What are you doing?' asked Miley.

'I'm looking for the dessicant spray.'

'There's none there. I used it.'

She paid no attention.

'Do you hear what I'm saying?' said Miley, growing annoyed. 'I used it all — burning off the spuds.'

'I know you're *supposed* to have used it. . . .'

'I'm *telling* you I did. . . .'

She turned on him.

'Well, why aren't the stalks burned off, then?'

Miley was taken aback.

'They must be.'

'Go and look at them!'

Biddy found a full container. She unscrewed the cap and sniffed at the contents.

Miley leaned forward and picked up another container. It was empty.

'Here, this was it.'

Biddy grabbed the empty container from him. She glared at it. Then she turned and glared at Miley.

'Is that what you put on the spuds?'

'Yeh.'

'*That's* fungicide. *This* one's the dessicant. You'd think by now you'd know the difference!'

She turned away from him and started to load the sprayer with the dessicant.

'Here,' said Miley. 'I'll do that.'

She continued working.

'Like you did it before?'

'All right,' said Miley. 'I made a mistake. . . .'

'You can say that again.'

'Let me do it,' said Miley.

'No,' she snapped at him. 'If I do it, at least I'll know it's done!'

Miley stared at her.

'Do you know what,' he said. 'You can be a right little bitch!'

He stalked away from her.

A short time later Mary and Carol found Biddy in the kitchen. She was crying.

'Biddy, what's the matter?' asked Mary anxiously.

Biddy made a great effort to regain her composure. She blew her nose.

'I can't go through with it,' she said.

'Now, now,' said her mother. 'Pull yourself together. Carol, make some tea.'

'I don't want tea!' Biddy screamed at her. 'I'm in desperation and all you can offer me is tea!'

'All right, take it easy. . . .'

Mary and Carol exchanged a quick glance.

'I can't marry him, Mam,' said Biddy. 'I just can't.'

They made the tea all the same. And Biddy drank a cup, becoming a little calmer as she did so.

'You see,' she said. 'Nothing's the same as it used to be.'

'Well,' said Carol, ' if you don't love him. . . .'

'But I *do*,' cried Biddy. 'I'm sure I do. I just can't see myself *married* to him.'

There was a knock at the outer door. Carol went to open it. Biddy dabbed hurriedly at her face, trying to wipe away the tears.

It was a very determined Miley who came in. Mary took one look at his expression and said,

'Come along, Carol. We've things to do.'

There was silence when they had gone. Miley remained standing, Biddy stayed sitting. Neither looked at the other.

Miley said, 'I thought maybe we should have a talk.'

'Talk away,' said Biddy.

'You're fighting a lot lately, so. . . .'

'It takes two.'

'All right,' said Miley. 'We're both fighting. But it's you that starts it.'

'It's not *me*.'

'It is so *you*.'

'Who put the fungicide on the Pinks?' said Biddy.

'That was a mistake,' said Miley. 'I had things on me mind.'

Biddy said sarcastically, 'You could've fooled me!'

There was a pause.

'Well, there you are,' said Miley.

She turned to scowl at him.

'What do you mean "there you are"?'

'You've started to fight again,' said Miley. 'Casting up fungicide. 'Tisn't fungicide I came here to talk about.'

'Well, what *did* you come to talk about?'

'It's . . . the way we're fighting.'

Biddy stood up angrily, knocking over her chair.

'We're just going round in circles,' she said.

She took her cup and saucer to the sink, clattering them noisily. Then she turned around to face him again.

'If you want to break it off, why don't you say so?'

'It isn't me that wants to break it off,' said Miley. 'It's yourself. There's a week to go. Plenty of time.'

'For what?'

'Putting it off. If that's what you want.'

'It seems to be what *you* want,' said Biddy.

'It is not. . . .'

'Well, you keep on about it,' said Biddy. 'I'm saying nothing more.'

'I'm saying nothing ayther,' said Miley.

He walked to the door. There he paused.

'Is it still on then?'

Biddy shrugged.

'I suppose so,' she said. 'No use in wasting the wedding dress.'

Miley nodded.

'Right so. I'll get on with the spraying.'

The moment he had left the room, Carol and Mary reappeared. Biddy was standing with her back to the sink, glowering at the floor.

'Well?' asked Mary.

'Well what?' said Biddy sullenly.

'Is it bad news?'

'Yeh.'

'You mean it's off?' said Carol.

'No,' said Biddy. 'It's on.'

And she banged out of the room, leaving Mary and Carol looking at each other in bewilderment.

That evening while Miley was staring gloomily into his pint at the bar of the Molly Malone, he was joined by George Manning.

'Well, Myles, old chap,' said George. 'You seem a little under the weather.'

'Aye,' said Miley.

'A touch of stage fright?' asked George.

'Ah no,' said Miley.

He became confidential.

'You see . . . This is between ourselves, George?'

'Of course, old man.'

Miley glanced cautiously around him before leaning his head close to George's.

'Tisn't me,' he said profoundly. 'Like, I feel exactly the same. No doubt in my mind at all at all. 'Tis Biddy.'

George nodded understandingly.

'She's desperate lately,' said Miley. 'You couldn't please her.'

'Hmm,' said George.

'Bag of weasels,' said Miley.

He returned to the gloomy contemplation of his pint.

'Of course,' said George, 'it *is* a very difficult time for a girl. The ah . . . the weaker vessel.'

The ghost of a smile crept through the gloom of Miley's face.

'Begod, George,' he said, 'I couldn't call Biddy the weaker anything.'

'Oh I quite agree,' said George. 'I was being jocular.'

Miley nodded.

'It's what my old commanding officer used to call his wife,' continued George. 'The weaker vessel. "The ladies are all right in their place," he used to say. "On the sidelines, cheering on the chaps. But not in the thick of things. The heavy infantry. Second row of the scrum." Of course, he was quite right. The heavy infantry and the second row of the scrum are for idiots.'

Miley looked puzzled.

'I'm not sure what you're saying, George.'

George coughed.

'I suppose I'm saying that women have a rather clearer view of things than my old commanding officer. So when they find themselves about to hand over a large part of their independence to people *like* my old commanding officer . . . Well, they tend to be filled with trepidation.'

'But I'm nothing like your old commanding officer,' said Miley.

'Of course not,' said George. 'He was quite small.'

'And I'm feeling a fair bit of trepidation meself.'

'Perfectly normal, old chap,' said George. 'Take these bachelor parties. I've been to dozens. They all pretend to be very jolly, last night of freedom, that sort of thing.'

It was George's turn to lower his voice.

'They're not in the least jolly, Myles.'

'Are they not?' said Miley.

George shook his head.

'Absolutely miserable, old chap. As if they were going into surgery. The drink is the anaesthetic.'

Meanwhile Biddy was in her kitchen, pouring tea for Uncle Peter. She added a dollop of whiskey to the cup.

'That'll liven it up for you,' said Biddy.

He smiled his little smile.

'You have me spoiled.'

He looked quizzically at her.

'You're in better form this evening,' he said.

'Why do you say that?'

'Last time I saw you,' said Peter, 'you were taking lumps out of poor Miley.'

'Won't do him a bit of harm,' said Biddy defiantly.

'Oh not a bit,' said Peter. 'Sure, you have to soften him up.'

'I wasn't softening . . .'

'Show him who's boss.'

She glared at him, but he merely smiled benignly back at her. Her glare melted a little.

'Is that what it looked like?'

Peter nodded.

'In fact, it might have been thought that you wanted to dump him altogether.'

'Well, I don't,' said Biddy.

There was a pause. Peter sipped his tea quietly. Then Biddy came to a decision.

'Uncle Peter, will you give me away at the wedding?'

He was very surprised.

'My father's dead, you see,' said Biddy. 'There's an uncle supposed to be doing it, but I hardly know him.'

'But sure, you don't know me at all,' said Peter.

'Indeed I do,' said Biddy. 'Will you do it?'

'I'd be honoured,' said Peter.

She kissed his cheek.

The next evening Miley drove the tractor up to the mushroom house, pulling a trailer loaded with potatoes. There was great activity. Girl mushroom-pickers were carrying chips of mushrooms to the cold-house. He switched off the engine and got down, just as Biddy came out carrying an armload of mushrooms. She walked down towards the cold-house. Miley followed her.

'How's it going inside?' he asked tentatively.

'All right,' said Biddy, equally tentatively.

She looked over at the trailer.

'You started the spuds?'

'Since half-six.'

He waited till she came out of the cold-house before he spoke again.

'I was thinking. . . .'

Biddy paused in her walk.

'Yeh?'

Miley tried to pick his words carefully.

'If you wanted to be left off the hook . . .'

'I don't.'

He tried again.

'But if you did, I wanted to say that's all right. It's all one.'

'What do you mean, it's all one?' There was more anxiety than snootiness in Biddy's voice.

'I mean if that's what you want . . .'

'I told you it's not!'

She came closer to him and looked up into his face.

'But I think it's what *you* want.'

'No,' said Miley shaking his head emphatically.

'Well, that's all right then,' said Biddy.

They stood close, looking at each other.

'What's the wedding dress like?' asked Miley.

'I didn't look,' said Biddy.

'Oh,' said Miley. Then, 'Well, I'll get on with the spuds.'

He turned away from her.

'Miley,' said Biddy.

He stopped.

'I *did* look,' said Biddy. 'It's lovely.'

He turned to face her again. She stepped forward and put her arms around him.

'I'm sorry, Miley.'

He clasped her awkwardly to his chest, patting her on the back.

'It's all right,' said Miley. 'It's all right.'

She raised her face to his and they kissed.

'I didn't mean any of it,' she said.

'I know you didn't,' said Miley. 'I know well. . . .'

Holding her in his arms he looked over her head and into the faces of giggling girls who were watching the romantic interlude.

'Ah here stop,' he said in alarm. 'They're all looking at us.'

Everything was better after that. The next day he even consented to go into Dublin to do some shopping with Biddy, Carol and Michelle Malone, Jack Malone's niece from the public house. Michelle and Carol were to be Biddy's bridesmaids.

Miley was in great form, despite being dragged around by three females. When they were walking down Grafton Street, he went into the swankiest shop he could find and asked where was the Butty Department.

The shop assistant stared at him.

'Butty Department?'

Miley pulled Biddy forward.

'For this little butty thing I'm going to be marrying next week.'

'Will you stop making a show of us!' said Biddy.

The girls bundled him out of the shop, all three of them laughing and pushing one another like children at a party.

Later on, when they announced that they were going to buy some lingerie, Miley detached himself from them and went to look for the shipping office.

Uncle Peter had told him that he was due to leave on another cruise the week after the wedding, and Miley thought he could save the old man some bother by checking the departure time for him.

And here he got a nasty shock. His enquiries at the shipping office were greeted with laughter. Oh, they knew Peter Donovan all right. But he was going on no cruise liner. In fact, he hadn't worked as a steward for over five years. Too old, they said. But he was always hanging around looking for a job he would never get.

'But how does he live?' asked Miley.

'Beats me,' said one of the clerks.

'Has he got a pension, or something?'

'He moved around too much. And dirtied his bib once too often. They gave him a lump sum five years ago, but that must be gone by now.'

And the 'nice little flat on the South Circular Road' which Peter so often talked about didn't exist either. Miley went to the address given him by the people in the shipping office, but he found only a shabby doss house. Yes, the manager said, Peter Donovan had been staying there off and on for the past five years.

It was a depressing shadow on an otherwise very happy day.

When Miley got home, he told Dinny and Biddy the news. As they were talking about it, Peter came in all smiles.

'Isn't that a grand evening?' he said. 'I brought you a few rashers for the tea.'

They were embarrassed, but Peter noticed nothing.

'Do you know my favourite food, Biddy?' he said. 'Couscous. I must show you how to make it. It's delicious. And the best place for it is Cairo.'

He rambled on, talking about his travels, and when Miley started to bring up the subject of the cruise liner, Dinny headed him off with a warning look. A sudden feeling of pity for the pretence of the little sailor overcame his natural aversion to the man.

'Nobody wants to hear what you were doing in Dublin today, Miley,' said Dinny.

'Sure, we can let him tell it anyway,' said Peter.

'We won't,' said Dinny. 'I've a sore head listening to him. What we'll do is, we'll have a little drink.'

And so it was left.

\*    \*    \*    \*    \*

On the morning of the wedding, Miley was up early and took out the tractor to lift the last of his potatoes. When he got back to the cottage, he found Peter and Dinny waiting for him, both of them resplendent in their hired morning suits.

'In the name of God, Miley,' said Dinny, 'what are you doing?'

'Finished them I did,' said Miley triumphantly. 'Every spud lifted. Do you know, Peter, if I hadn't've finished the spuds it would have cast a shadow on the wedding. I'd've gone through the honeymoon wondering about the spuds.'

'All right, now,' said Dinny. 'Do you think you might come in and put on the wedding suit.'

'No,' said Miley, making for the door. 'I'm going up to Matt's house for a proper bath. I want the shower and the loofah brush and the herbal shampoo and the pumice stone for scraping the feet. This is no day for taking chances.'

'Hold on,' said Dinny.

He went into the bedroom and returned with a supermarket shopping bag.

'What's this?' asked Miley.

'Clane vest and underpants,' said Dinny. 'There's nothing worse than having a bath and climbing into dirty drawers.'

'Right,' said Miley.

He got into his van and drove off.

In the MacDermott house all was chaos. There were clothes all over the place. Carol was ironing her dress and Michelle was putting make-up on Biddy. Mary was doing her best to keep everyone sane and on course by cooking some breakfast.

Auntie Florrie came into the kitchen.

'Do you know Miley's after driving away in his van?' she said.

'I hope he remembers what day it is,' said Carol.

'He's probably going to set up a vegetable stall in front of the church,' Mary laughed. 'Come on, everybody, sit over to the table.'

'What way is Miley getting to the church?' asked Michelle.

'I bet you anything you like he's going to come in the van,' said Biddy.

'Ah he wouldn't!'

'He would of course,' said Biddy.

'Don't worry about it,' said Mary. 'I'll talk to him.'

But in the heel of the hunt, Miley *did* go to the church in the van. Matt Moran was to have taken Dinny and himself, but Matt's car broke down, as it usually did, and Miley drove his father and his best man into Glenroe.

The church was full for the ceremony. Biddy walked in on Peter's arm and everybody said how well she looked. Father Devereux officiated. There were no last minute hitches. Matt had the ring ready when it was needed and Father Devereux gave only the slightest look of disapproval when he saw the cut of Matt's fingers, which still bore the oily marks he had got while trying to get his car to go. Father Devereux gave the ring a rub on his surplice before handing it on to Miley to place on Biddy's finger.

The reception was held in Clouseau's Restaurant. After the meal Matt read the telegrams, which contained the usual mixture of sincere, solemn messages and fatuous jokes. When he had finished, he gathered up the telegrams and placed them in a neat little pile. He tapped his glass for silence.

'And now,' he began, ' it is my pleasure to call on Mister . . .'

Miley was on his feet in an instant.

'Ah hold on, Matt,' he said. 'Hold on. If you don't mind me butting in.'

He put a large hand on Matt's shoulder and gently forced him to sit down. Then Miley faced the crowd.

'The last wedding I was at,' he said, 'I was the best man and I remember sitting up half the night with the book of etiquette, learning it all off. The father of the bride was to propose the toast of the happy couple. The groom had to respond on behalf of the bride and propose the toast of the bridesmaids. And then the best man had to respond on behalf of the bridesmaids. There was nobody allowed to speak for themselves at all at all. Anyway, I promised meself that if ever I got married there'd be none of that oul cod. It's *my* wedding. . . .'

Biddy gave a loud cough. A titter ran through the audience. Miley grinned.

'*And* Biddy's. It's *our* wedding. And there's only going to be one speech — and this is it! So Matt Moran and Father Devereux and Uncle Peter and me father — especially me father — can hold onto their speeches for another occasion.'

This brought another round of applause.

'So it's up to me,' continued Miley, ' to thank everybody. And that's as it should be, because it's me that's getting the best bargain.'

It was as near as Miley could ever get to being maudlin. Biddy looked suitably pleased and dewy-eyed and Mary had her own hand-kerchief out. There was further applause.

'Well now,' said Miley. 'The bridesmaids, of course. Carol and Michelle. They'll be the next to go. Father Devereux . . . you did the job well, Father. There'll be no getting out of it. Uncle Peter took the time off from travelling round the world to come and give away the bride. You'll always be welcome, Peter.'

Peter smiled his benign little smile, nodding all about him as the guests applauded him. Dinny rolled his eyes to heaven.

'Then there was the best man, Matt. I'm very grateful to you, Matt, for keeping me right,' said Miley. 'Only one thing I'd ask you. Would you in the name of God get yourself a new car!'

Matt grinned. Father Devereux gave an approving nod.

Miley became more serious.

'To Biddy's mother,' he said, 'and to her late father, I owe the most of all. It must have been very hard over the past year to put up with the like of me all the time on the doorstep. Mind you, they didn't bring up Biddy very well. She can be very impudent. But I'll knock that out of her, never fear.'

This brought hoots of derision and a sharp poke in the ribs from Biddy.

Dick Moran leaned across to Mary and whispered in her ear.

'There's an innocent poor slob, if ever I saw one.'

'Still and all,' Miley went on, 'no matter what trouble I have in the years to come keeping Biddy in order, it'll be nothing to the job I've had this past thirty-seven years looking after me father.'

There were more cheers.

'Will you listen to the impertinence of that!' said Dinny.

'In spite of that,' said Miley across to him, 'I'm grateful for all he's done for me. And for his help in making the match. And I'm eternally grateful to someone else that nobody here except meself and me father and Uncle Peter had the good luck to know. And that was me mother.'

He paused a moment. The whole room grew very quiet.

'Last of all,' said Miley, 'I want to thank Biddy.'

He looked down at her and she looked up to meet his eyes.

'For having me,' said Miley.

He sat down. Biddy took his hand and held it tightly. Champagne corks popped and everyone stood up to toast the bride and groom.

Later, Miley came downstairs. He had changed into a new suit. He bumped into Mary and grabbed her by the arm.

'Listen till I tell you,' he said. 'The compost won't arrive till the morning after we're due back. That's the Friday. Now, if we're not back on time on the Thursday, you have to get the spent compost out of number three house and get it well washed. Do you hear me?'

'Yes, Miley, I know all that,' said Mary patiently.

'Now, the new stuff has to go in very quick, so I've told Stephen Brennan . . .'

'Miley, I know all about it,' said Mary.

'Now, I've worked out there shouldn't be any big flush in the week we're away,' said Miley, ignoring her interruption, 'but if there is, you're to be sure to give them a good watering and then . . .'

A huge cheer went up. Biddy, now wearing her going-away outfit, had appeared on the stairs. Mary escaped from Miley and went to join her. Biddy raised her bouquet. There were more cheers as she threw it down to the crowd gathered in the foyer. It was caught by Michelle. A widely grinning Matt Moran thought that this was most appropriate.

Miley had now buttonholed Dinny.

'Now, when Nuala comes,' said Miley, 'you're to make her take all the carrots you can and all the cabbage too. Then all the spuds have to be bagged and . . .'

'Aye, right, right, right, I hear you,' said Dinny.

He broke away from Miley and went to kiss the bride. Stephen Brennan appeared at Miley's elbow. He had the newspaper in his hand.

'Did you see this, Miley?' he asked. 'About the price of mushrooms.'

Miley took the paper from him and began to study it intently. Mary came over, took Miley's arm and pulled him towards the door.

'Come on now, Miley,' she said. 'You're going to miss your plane.'

Miley, even as he was being ushered out into the car, continued to read the paper. When they finally had said all their goodbyes and were safely on their way to the airport, he turned to his new bride.

'Did you see what it said in the paper?' he asked her.

'When would I get time to see the paper!'

'The price of mushrooms is up to eighty-five pence a pound, due to a severe shortage on the English market.'

'That's great,' said Biddy, with no more interest than if he were talking about juvenile delinquency in Outer Mongolia.

'Do you know what I'm going to tell you?' said Miley. '*That's* going to make my holiday.'

# · CHAPTER NINE ·

# MICHELLE

The first person Michelle Malone saw when she got off the train in Glenroe was the handsome young man with the dark hair and flashing white teeth. His skin was so tanned she wondered if he was an Arab Sheik over in Ireland to buy a couple of hotels and maybe fall in love with her and carry her off on his camel, and she nearly fell out of her standing when he came up to her and said her name.

'Michelle?'

'Yeh?' said Michelle.

'Your Uncle Jack sent me to meet you,' said the young man.

'Oh,' said Michelle.

So he wasn't an Arab Sheik. But he was nice all the same. He picked up her huge case and they walked out of the station together.

'You're not me cousin, are you?' asked Michelle.

'No, no.'

'Well, who are you?'

'Oh sorry,' said the young man. 'Matt Moran.'

He put down her case and they solemnly shook hands. He picked up the case again. It was very heavy.

'What's in the bag?'

'Weights,' said Michelle.

'Oh,' said Matt.

'I do weight training,' said Michelle.

Well, it wasn't really a lie. She always wanted to do weight training, but she just never had the chance.

She wasn't very impressed with the car Matt was driving. It wasn't one of the big limos an Arab would have had. And it took a bit of starting up too. She sat in the passenger seat, looking small and pale and vulnerable while he fought with the engine. A camel would have gone much easier.

He took her to the MacDermott house first, where she was to stay, and then down to the Molly Malone where her Uncle Jack was the owner. Aunty Molly had gone off and left him, which was why Michelle had been sent for, to give him a helping hand in the pub.

Well, it wasn't quite like that really. Her mother thought maybe if she was down in a back-of-the-pipes place like Glenroe she'd be out of harm's way. Fat chance.

That night she found herself telling Biddy and Mary that her father was an alcoholic.

'Never touched a drop till he was forty-five,'said Michelle. 'And then he tried a glass of champagne at a wedding. That was the end of him.'

'Is he dead?' asked Mary.

'No . . . he's in a place . . . you know . . .'

'An institution?'

'Yeh, that's right.'

As she lay in bed later on she grinned to herself, thinking what her father would say if he knew the yarns she'd been spinning about him.

She went to work in the pub the next day. And young Matt Moran turned up, just to see her. He drove her home that night. He said her Uncle Jack had asked him to take her under his wing, but Michelle knew that he was doing it because he liked her. She liked him too. He was easy to get on with and he was very obliging.

About a week later he kissed her. It happened while they were sitting in his car after he had driven her back from the pub.

'Thanks for bringing me home,' said Michelle.

'I suppose you're wondering why I wasn't in the pub the past couple of nights,' said Matt. 'I've moved into this new house, you see. Lots of jobs to do.'

'I'm sorry for dragging you out.'

'No, I was glad of the excuse,' said Matt.

'Must be nice,' said Michelle wistfully. 'A place of your own.'

Matt looked puzzled.

'You live with your parents, don't you?'

'They're not really my parents,' said Michelle. 'I'm adopted.'

'Oh,' said Matt.

'I wasn't told till I was fourteen,' said Michelle, warming to the story. 'I tried to trace them, but the trail was cold.'

'Did you not find *anything*'

'Oh I did, a little bit,' said Michelle. 'Me father was a foreign diplomat and he met me mother when he was over in his embassy in Dublin.'

'And your mother was Irish?' asked Matt.

'Yeh, she was,' said Michelle. 'She was a dancer. I'm supposed to be like her. But, you see, me father was recalled back to his own country and me mother never wrote to him in case it might ruin his career. And she couldn't keep a child because she was always travelling, so she put me for adoption. I was three years in St. Philomena's Orphanage.'

Matt took her hand and she raised her big eyes to his.

'Maybe I should go in now,' said Michelle.

'In a minute,' said Matt.

And that was when he kissed her.

The next night she arrived at the house alone.

'Is Matt not with you?' asked Biddy.

'He ran me as far as the gate,' said Michelle.

'Why didn't he come in?'

'I said I was washing me hair,' said Michelle.

Biddy grinned at her and Michelle grinned back.

'You have him like a lapdog,' said Biddy.

'Yeh, I know.'

'Do you like him?'

'Oh I do,' said Michelle. 'Like, he's very biddable.'

And she did really like him and not just because he was biddable. She occasionally wondered what he'd say if he knew that she wasn't illegitimate, that she wasn't adopted, that her father and her mother kept a sweet shop in Sallynoggin, and that they were both lifelong Pioneers. But she didn't tell him. He'd find out soon enough and she could worry about it then.

She kept promising herself that she wouldn't tell any more stories, but before she knew it she was off again. Sometimes she was amazed at the things she heard herself saying.

Like the night in the pub just before Biddy and Miley got married. Father Devereux had come in for his bottle of oloroso and he stopped to have a little chat with her.

'Isn't it a wonder your Uncle Jack never had you down before this,' he said.

'Ah well, he couldn't,' said Michelle. 'Up to a year ago.'

'You were at school, were you?'

Michelle leaned forward and lowered her voice.

'I was a postulant.'

'Were you now!' said Devereux in surprise. 'Where was this?'

'In Switzerland,' said Michelle.

'What part?'

'In the mountains,' said Michelle.

'Yes,' said the priest. 'But was it French-speaking? Or German? Or Italian?

Michelle thought for a moment.

'It was different languages different days,' she said at last.

'And you had to learn them all?' said Devereux, looking at her in admiration.

'No,' said Michelle. 'You see, we didn't speak. We had a vow of silence.'

Devereux was very impressed.

'And how long were you there?'

'Eight years,' said Michelle. 'I was fourteen when I entered.'

'And you never spoke for eight years?'

'Only me prayers,' said Michelle.

'God bless us and save us,' said Devereux.

He wandered out of the pub in a sort of daze.

*   *   *   *   *

Biddy asked her to be a bridesmaid at her wedding and Michelle caught the bouquet, which pleased Matt very much.

Things were getting very serious between them. They had moved a long way from that first chaste kiss in the car and now both of them found themselves deeply in love for the first time. Every available minute they could get off from work they spent together, sometimes walking by the river, sometimes in Matt's house, when his brother, Paul, wasn't at home.

Matt, of course, found out about her stories — Uncle Jack was going around warning everybody not to believe a word out of her mouth — but Matt didn't really seem to mind.

One day he raised the subject. They were walking by the river at the time. Michelle was feeling a bit woebegone, but Matt didn't seem to notice. Every now and again he stopped and kissed her. Eventually they reached their favourite spot and Matt put his raincoat on the grass and they sat down.

There was silence for a little while. Michelle looked at the water and wondered how she was going to tell him. She opened her mouth to speak, but he got in before she could.

'Michelle,' he said, 'why do you tell stories?'

'Are you going to give out to me again?'

'No, I'm just curious,' said Matt. 'I mean, this latest one.'

'What one?'

'About the convent in the Swiss Alps.'

'Oh yeh,' said Michelle, remembering Father Devereux's face.

'Jack was very annoyed,' said Matt.

'Yeh, I know.'

'So why do you do it?'

Michelle thought about it.

'Some of the things,' she said, 'I have them out before I know what I'm saying. And then . . . well, it's like trying out new paint on a wall. Once you've started, you've got to keep going.'

Matt smiled fondly at her.

'Maybe you should be writing books.'

'I *did* write a book,' said Michelle. 'People said I ought to publish it, but I wouldn't. It was too private.'

Matt was looking at her sceptically.

'Well, I *started* to write it,' said Michelle.

He just shook his head in loving amusement.

'You're really something else,' he said.

There was a silence for a few moments. Matt picked up some pebbles and began throwing them into the water. She felt that this was the proper time to tell him.

'Matt . . .' said Michelle.

'Yeh?'

'I've something to tell you.'

'Sounds bad,' said Matt, throwing another stone.

'I'm pregnant,' said Michelle.

He turned his head to look at her. Then he turned away and continued throwing the pebbles.

'Did you hear me?' asked Michelle.

'Yeh, I heard.'

'You sound as if you don't care,' said Michelle.

Matt turned again to face her.

'Oh I'd care all right,' he said. 'If it was true.'

'But it *is* true!'

'Yeh.'

'I'm telling you the truth,' wailed Michelle.

But he wouldn't believe her. Even Biddy didn't believe her when Michelle told her that night.

'How do you know?' asked Biddy.

'The doctor told me,' said Michelle.

'What doctor?'

'I forget his name,' said Michelle angrily. 'And you're just trying to catch me out, asking what doctor.'

'Well,' said Biddy, when she was finally convinced, 'the one you want to persuade is Matt. And there's only one way to do that — bring him to the doctor.'

Matt turned out to be delighted at the news. Of course, there was the first shock, which rocked him a bit, but after that he took to the idea like a duck to water. He hugged her as they came out of the

141

doctor's surgery and insisted that they should go immediately and tell his father.

Dick Moran was surprised, but he knew too much about the world to be overwhelmed by anything of that nature.

'Have you told your parents?' he asked. 'Or Jack?'

'I'm telling him tonight,' said Michelle.

She turned her big soulful eyes up to him.

'I'm sorry, Mr Moran.'

'It's not the end of the world, Michelle,' said Dick, smiling at her. 'It's happened before and it'll happen again. Tell me, for a start . . . are you going to *have* the baby?'

'Yeh . . .' said Michelle.

'Course we are!' said Matt.

'Good,' said Dick.

'I think we ought to get married as soon as possible,' said Matt.

Michelle looked at him in surprise.

'We haven't really talked about it,' she said.

Later, when they were alone, she had a very troubled air about her.

'What's wrong with you?' asked Matt.

'We never said anything about getting married, Matt,' she said.

'But why delay?' said Matt. 'I mean, we love each other. . . .'

'Yeh, I know all that,' said Michelle. 'I just don't know if getting married is a good idea.'

'But it's all set,' said Matt. 'I've got the house, Paul says he wants to move out, so we have a place all to ourselves to move into straight-away.'

'Yeh, I know,' said Michelle. 'I really like the house. And I *do* love you, Matt. . . .'

'So what's the problem?'

'There's no problem about me moving into the house,' said Michelle. 'Or about me having the baby. Or about the two of us looking after it together. . . .'

Matt put his arms around her, but she held him off.

'I just don't think I want to get married,' said Michelle.

\*     \*     \*     \*     \*

They didn't get married. Despite Matt's urgent appeals, which continued off and on for months, Michelle set her face firmly against the idea. But she moved into the house with him and they found that they got on very well together. It was a bit like the games they used to play when they were children.

A worried Miley Byrne.

'These pair are champions or my name isn't Dinny Byrne.'

'Look, Stephen, I don't see what the problem is.'

'Yes, Mrs McDaid, I quite understand.'

Sergeant Roche keeps a keen eye on proceedings.

Teasy enjoys a joke.

'And a Happy Christmas to you too, Stephen.'

Kevin puts Michelle and Teasy in the picture.

Dick tries to reason with James O'Driscoll.

'Well now, Stephen, as you and Dick both know I have no say in the matter.'

Denise's teething has both Biddy and Miley up during the night.

Biddy, Miley and a sleeping Denise.

The Byrne women on Denise's first birthday.

Matt began to get very domesticated. He was always going into other houses and looking at the wallpaper and asking who did the kitchen and things like that. Then he'd drag her round to shops to look at patterns and colour schemes. She put up with this as best she could, though she wasn't really interested. One wallpaper was very much like another.

They were sitting at home one evening. Matt had been looking very thoughtful altogether and she asked him what was on his mind.

'I was talking to Stephen Brennan today. He said that Nuala is all excited about her new baby.'

'Well, of course, she's excited,' said Michelle. 'I'm excited about mine.'

'Yeh, but that's just the point,' said Matt. 'Nuala can go around talking about it to everybody she meets.'

'So can I.'

'No, you can't,' said Matt. 'Not really.'

'Well . . .' said Michelle. 'Sure, can't I talk to *you*?'

'Yeh. . . .'

However, he didn't seem all that convinced.

A few days later, as Michelle was walking up the street, she saw Matt's car parked outside his father's office, so she turned in through the door to say hello to him. She was just in time to find Matt and Father Devereux in some sort of a confrontation. Matt was looking very cross about something and Devereux seemed embarrassed to see her.

'Is anything wrong?' she asked.

'Look, Matt,' said Devereux, 'none of this is turning out the way it was meant. I'll go now and we'll talk later.'

'No, wait, Father,' said Matt. 'You have the two of us now. You can say what you came to say.'

Father Devereux looked at Michelle.

'I don't think Matt's in a proper mood to talk to anybody, so . . .'

'If you have something to say to me you should say it,' said Matt, sounding very masculine and strong. 'You didn't have to go to my father first!'

'Father's only doing his job,' said Michelle gently.

'Maybe another time,' said Devereux.

He opened the door to leave. Matt cooled down considerably, more like the Matt she knew.

'I'm sorry if I seemed rude, Father,' he said.

'Perfectly all right,' said Devereux. 'Could I just ask you one thing? I'm not trying to read the Riot Act. I'm not even asking as a priest. I'm just curious. You seem genuinely fond of each other. Why don't you marry? Do it the right way?'

'We might still,' said Matt. 'But everybody's always saying that young people shouldn't rush into marriage.'

'And I think that's good advice,' said Devereux.

'Why?' asked Michelle.

'Because it's a commitment for life,' said Devereux. 'They can't afford to make mistakes.'

'But that's what *we* say,' said Michelle. 'I mean, all right I did wrong getting pregnant. That was one mistake we rushed into. We're not going to rush into another.'

'Don't worry, Father,' said Matt. 'We're staying together.'

Father Devereux nodded resignedly.

'The minute you decide you'd like to get married,' he said, 'I want you to come and see me. The two of you.'

'Might be three of us,' said Matt.

'I wanted to ask you that, Father,' said Michelle. 'Will there be any trouble about baptizing the child?'

'No,' said Devereux emphatically. 'Why should there be!'

\*     \*     \*     \*     \*

Chuck Boyle started to come into the pub. He was a big, brawny young man of twenty-one, who had been hired by Biddy and Miley to look after the mushrooms for them. One of a large and poor family, he was determined to get on in the world. He told Michelle that nobody ever got rich working for a wage and that he was going to have his own business one day.

Michelle liked him from the start. He was always very quiet and spent most of his spare time studying books, but when he came into the pub for a pint at the end of the day, he often chatted to Michelle and they got along well together.

Matt got a bit jealous of the newcomer, even though there was no need. Michelle didn't mind him being jealous — it livened things up. Anyway, whenever there was a bit of a tiff about it, there was always a nice making-up time afterwards.

Then one evening, about a month before the baby was due, Michelle found herself rushing along the road, late for work. Chuck came by on his motorbike and she persuaded him, against his better judgement, to give her a lift on the pillion.

They were going around a bend in the road, when they were confronted by a car coming towards them on its wrong side. Chuck braked and pulled into the ditch, but the car struck the back wheel of the bike and Michelle was flung off onto the road. She was knocked unconscious and was taken off to hospital in an ambulance.

When Matt arrived at the scene of the accident, he jumped at Chuck and knocked him down.

Michelle didn't hear about the fight till later on. She was much too busy having her baby. A little boy, tiny but perfect, was born to her. As she explained to Biddy later, she didn't like Ricky all that much at the start and for nearly a month afterwards, but he gradually wormed his way into her affections.

Matt, who had spent anxious hours waiting for news from the hospital, loved his son immediately. Michelle's mother, Lily Malone, arrived out from Sallynoggin, to be with her poor misfortunate daughter. Despite the unmistakeable presence of Matt, and even when she was directly addressing him, Lily kept referring to the baby as the 'poor fatherless child'. She told both of the young parents that they were going to get married now, or she'd take mother and child back home with her.

But Michelle remained adamant that she didn't think they were ready for marriage yet. Lily had to be content with the fact that the baby was properly christened in the church and she consoled herself that Michelle was probably only going through a 'phrase.' She stayed with them the night after the christening, but insisted that Matt sleep on the sofa.

'I'm not sleeping in any house,' said Lily, 'where me daughter is sleeping with a man that's not her husband.'

'What do you think happens when you're not here?' said Michelle.

'I try not to think about it,' said Lily.

Whatever her mother may have thought about the domestic arrangements, Michelle and Matt blossomed into competent parents. Ricky was very well looked after most of the time. However, there was one incident which caused a lot of trouble.

It happened on a day that Michelle had been invited to lunch by Biddy. She rushed into the pub, late as usual, to buy a bottle of wine to take with her. She had Ricky with her in his carrycot. George Manning was behind the bar, filling in as temporary barman, something which he quite enjoyed and did as often as he was permitted. While George was wrapping the bottle of wine, Michelle dashed into the ladies' room to do her face. She emerged a few minutes later, looked at the clock, gave a gasp of dismay, grabbed the bottle of wine from George, and ran out of the pub.

She missed the bus out to Biddy's place, but was lucky enough to get a lift from Paul Moran. When she got to the house she found Biddy, Miley and Matt waiting for her, and the food being kept hot in the oven. She was profuse in her apologies.

'Michelle . . .' said Matt.

Michelle held out the bottle of wine to Biddy.

'Oh, this is for you,' she said. 'Can I do anything to help?'

Matt's voice was now considerably louder.

'Michelle,' he said, 'where's the baby?'

Michelle stared at him in sudden dismay.

When they got back to the pub, Uncle Peter was feeding the baby from a bottle.

'Ah, Michelle,' said George, 'I think you left something.'

Matt grabbed the bottle and the baby from Peter. He was furious.

'What's in this?' he snapped.

'Diet tonic water,' said George.

'He appeared to like it,' said Uncle Peter with his warm little smile.

Matt put the bottle and the baby in the carrycot and strode out of the bar without as much as a glance at Michelle.

'He's very annoyed,' said Michelle to George.

'Yes, I think he may be,' said George sympathetically.

'It just slipped me mind,' said Michelle. 'Sure, it could happen to anybody.'

Matt crashed the door open.

'Are you coming?' he shouted.

'Yeh,' said Michelle.

She turned to Peter and George.

'Thanks for minding him.'

Matt was very annoyed, all right. For days afterwards he was very quiet and morose, not quite sullen, but near enough. When she questioned him about the fact that he didn't speak half the time they were together, he got uptight.

'It's not the baby,' he said. 'It's us. It's the whole thing. It's all wrong.'

'You want to split up?' asked Michelle anxiously

'No!' he said. 'It's just the opposite. We should get married. Other people do.'

'Look at other people,' said Michelle. 'Look at your own father.'

'He can't wait to get married to Mary MacDermott,' said Matt, as if that proved everything.

'Yeh,' said Michelle. 'He couldn't wait the first time either. Took him ten weeks to get married and twenty years to escape. In fact, he's still waiting for a lot of oul fellas in Rome to tell him what to do with his life. Well, they're not going to tell *me*!'

'I've got a say in this,' said Matt.

'Do you not *see*?' said Michelle. 'We're together now because we *want* to be . . . not because we *have* to be. Can't you see that?'

Maybe it was then that things started to go wrong. Oh there was no big row, no flare up, just a gradual sort of a drift from happiness into something else. He began to stay away from home a lot. He seldom came to pick her up at the pub. When they *were* together, sometimes whole evenings would go over with very little talk between them.

Finally came the day when Matt announced that he was moving out. He took her down to his brother Paul, the solicitor, and drew up an agreement whereby Michelle and Ricky could remain in the house for as long as they wished. There was also a generous sum for maintenance, which Matt guaranteed to pay every month. Dick Moran wasn't at all happy at the financial arrangements, but Matt stuck to his guns.

He wasn't a bad lad, thought Michelle, even though she felt she should have been hating him for abandoning Ricky and herself. She cried a lot at first. There were nights when she hardly slept at all, what with having to get up to Ricky and then weeping into her pillow when she got back into bed again, nights when she felt that the whole world was tumbling down about her ears. But that eventually passed and she settled down in her practical way to get on with the business of living and rearing her son.

# · CHAPTER TEN ·

# TEASY'S MEN

'Promise me one thing,' the Monsignor had whispered, turning himself painfully in the bed. 'Promise me that you'll do nothing with it for at least six months.'

It was an easy promise to make. What in the name of heaven would she be doing with it anyway! She had never been used to anything like it. And she was no fool. There was no complacency in that description of herself; it was no more than the plain truth. Teasy MacDaid had her head screwed on the right way round.

When she met Dinny Byrne she liked him. He seemed a kindly man, with a natural warmth. The minute he heard about her situation, he offered to bring her back to Glenroe, as if it were the most natural thing in the world to take a perfect stranger into his home, no questions asked, simply because she had worked for his brother and he had known her sister for a short time before her death.

Teasy liked him, but she felt he was a man who could do with a fair bit of watching. In the best possible way, of course. He had a gamey eye.

She liked Miley even better when she met him at the airport. The big gormless innocence of the man appealed to the mother in her and his easy acceptance of the situation warmed her heart.

'Sure, of course Biddy'll be delighted,' he assured her.

'I don't know,' said Teasy. 'Coming in on top of her without any warning . . . Would you not ring her, even?'

'No need,' said Dinny. 'She'll take it in her stride.'

'I'm telling you, now,' said Miley. 'Don't you give it another thought.'

So she sat back in the car, listening to Dinny praising the breakfast that Biddy would have ready for them, and watched the changing panorama as they drove through Dublin, across the Liffey and out through the south suburbs to Bray and beyond.

Glenroe looked a tidy little village. She saw a modernistic church and a pub called The Molly Malone — she liked that! Then the car swung into a narrow lane and pulled up before a neat, well-kept bungalow.

Dinny was out of the car like a shot and trundled in ahead of Miley, who was carrying the bags.

'Where is she at all?' Dinny was shouting inside in the house.

'I'm here', said a woman's voice.

Teasy marched in behind them. Dinny was hugging a young woman. He became aware that the young woman was staring over his shoulder at Teasy, so he released her and turned around. A bit uneasily, Teasy thought.

'You see, Biddy, I'm not alone . . .'

'Biddy, is it?' said Teasy.

'Yes. . . .' said Biddy, doubtfully, her eyes taking in the mohair sweater and leather trousers. Despite her promise to the Monsignor, Teasy had splashed a bit on new clothes for the journey home.

'I've heard all about you, love,' said Teasy. 'And who's this?'

She turned to the little man who was sitting at the table. He smiled a benign smile.

'This is me brother-in-law, Peter Donovan,' said Dinny, not very enthusiastically.

'Howrya, Peter. Don't get up.'

She said this only to be polite, because Peter showed no signs of stirring himself. Teasy looked around at the bright room.

'Well, isn't this nice!' she said. 'I suppose you're asking yourself who in the name of God I am?'

'I was kinda wondering all right,' Biddy said

'Maybe you thought I was a hitch-hiker,' said Teasy.

'Actually, Biddy,' said Dinny, 'this is Teasy.'

'Teasy MacDaid,' says Teasy cheerfully. 'I feel terrible barging in on you without warning. . . .'

'Ah sure, it's no problem in the wide earthly world,' said Miley.

'Dinny here's been making me mouth water all the way from Dublin,' said Teasy, 'talking about the breakfast you're going to have for us, with the back rashers and the black and white puddens. And it smells great. What do you say, Peter?'

'Oh sure you couldn't whack it,' said the little man.

'Do you know I haven't had a decent breakfast for six months. Nothing but pancakes and maple syrup and little streaky rashers only fit for putting on the turkey at Christmas,' said Teasy. 'Tell us, where's the powder room?'

'It's just at the end of the hall,' said Biddy.

Teasy felt that Dinny had some explaining to do to Biddy for landing this stranger in on top of her and she wanted to be out of the room while all that was going on.

When Dinny had travelled over to New England to attend the funeral of his brother, Father Jim, the Monsignor, he had discovered

Teasy MacDaid reluctantly holding down the job of housekeeper. Teasy had gone out there six months previously at the request of her sister, Essie, who had been Father Jim's housekeeper for forty years. Finding herself in bad health, Essie had asked Teasy to look after the Monsignor when she died and Teasy had done so, for Essie's sake. But the Monsignor had survived his housekeeper by only six months.

Teasy could have stayed on with the new Parish Priest had she so wished, but she was fed up with ironing canonicals and keeping her conversation respectable and she wanted to return to Ireland.

When she came back into the kitchen, she found that at least some explanations had been made.

'Dinny says you'll be staying with us,' said Biddy. She didn't sound overjoyed at the prospect.

'Yeah,' said Teasy. 'Isn't he an oul dote!'

'He's a sweetheart,' said Biddy with no expression on her face.

Teasy decided to let it ride for the minute. She sniffed at the frying rashers.

'Oh, isn't that a massive smell!'

'I'll take your cases down to your room,' said Miley.

'When you come back,' Biddy said to him, 'would you keep an eye on the rashers? I'll be outside with your father.'

Biddy left the room with a nod to Dinny to follow her. He did so very reluctantly. Miley took the cases and went out the other door. Teasy automatically took over the cooking.

'Aren't they a lovely family?' she said to Peter as she turned the rashers in the pan.

'They are surely,' said Peter. 'Doctor Barnado's wouldn't be in it.'

Miley returned.

'There you are now,' he said. 'I've left the cases on the bed.'

'Lovely,' said Teasy. 'Now Miley we have to settle the rent.'

'Will you go ower that — there'll be no rent.'

'Oh I'll sort it out with Biddy,' said Teasy. 'I can see you're no businessman. Peter, do you take one egg, or two?'

'Three,' said the little man.

After breakfast, Dinny brought Teasy over to Stephen Brennan's Farm shop. Stephen was up a ladder hanging hanks of onions from the ceiling.

'This is me old sparring partner, Stephen Brennan,' said Dinny. 'I've someone here I want you to meet, Stephen.'

Stephen came down the ladder in jig-time. He was wearing a shop-coat and a cap and he had a nice little moustache. He beamed at Teasy.

'You mean this beautiful woman is with *you*?' he said.

'Teasy MacDaid, late of Boston, Massachusetts,' said Dinny.

'Oh stop the lights,' said Stephen. He stuck out his hand. 'Stephen Brennan, late of Ballygannon, Glenroe, County Wicklow.'

They shook hands.

'Are you here on your holidays?' asked Stephen.

'Indeed I'm not,' said Teasy. 'Dinny brought me home and I'm home for keeps.'

Stephen's eyes widened and he turned to stare at Dinny. Teasy grinned at him and walked around the shop, picking out some vegetables. She had her ears pricked up and she caught the exchange between the two men, even though they kept their voices down.

'Are you taking the big step, Dinny?'

'Are you joking me!'

Teasy smiled quietly to herself. She bought a big boxful of vegetables to bring back to Biddy.

That evening, after dinner, Teasy insisted on doing the dishes with Biddy.

'You're steeped with that husband of yours,' said Teasy. 'Do you know that?'

'Yeh, I know,' said Biddy. 'Is your own husband dead?'

Teasy decided to stick to her usual story.

'Ten years,' she said.

'Do you miss him?'

'No,' said Teasy emphatically. 'God forgive me for saying it, but he was a proper louser.'

'You might have better luck next time,' said Biddy.

Teasy grinned and shook her head.

'No way,' she said. 'There'll be no next time. Now, listen, we have to fix the rent. Is fifty a week all right?'

'Teasy, I don't want rent,' said Biddy.

'I always work me corner and I always pay me way,' said Teasy.

'Well, fifty's far too much . . .'

Teasy dried her hands and took out her chequebook.

'I can't give you any less.'

'And all the shopping you brought in,' said Biddy. 'I wouldn't buy that much in a month. You shouldn't throw your money around like that.'

Teasy was busily writing out the cheque. She wanted to tell Biddy that the money didn't matter a damn, but she held her tongue.

'I was never able to hold on to money,' she said, 'and it never worried me. If I had it, all right, and if I hadn't, that was all right too.'

She tore out the cheque and handed it to Biddy.

'That's for a month in advance.'

Teasy liked the atmosphere in the Molly Malone. She hadn't been wrong about the pub. And she liked the people she met there — Jack Malone, the owner, and Biddy's mother and her intended, Dick Moran. Stephen Brennan was there too, but his mood wasn't the best. His wife, Nancy, was sick in hospital. Teasy dragged him into the group and insisted on buying him a drink.

'Tell us, Jack,' she said to the publican. 'Do you ever have a game of cards? Like poker?'

'Not here.'

'Have you no back room?'

'Only the kitchen. And it's in a desperate state.'

'Sure, that's easy fixed,' said Teasy. 'Show us it.'

In no time, she had them all organised, a table laid out, ham sandwiches on the dresser and a group ready and willing to take part.

But at the last moment there came the news that Nancy Brennan had died.

\*    \*    \*    \*    \*

In the weeks that followed, when the funeral was over and things were getting back to normal, Teasy got the poker school up and running. The only fly in the ointment was Uncle Peter, who consistently proclaimed his ignorance of the game, but just as consistently turned up 'three little aces' or 'a tiny bit of a flush' at those crucial times when the kitty was full and the betting heavy. However, this was a small price to pay for many pleasant evenings — until the sergeant put an end to the school by raiding the pub and catching them all, even Father Devereux, up to their ears in it.

By this time, out of consideration for Biddy, Teasy had transferred herself to the vacant flat over the pub, and Dick and Mary had officially announced their engagement.

And it was during the party to celebrate this event that Matt Moran arrived with the news that Jack Malone was on one of his periodic skites. This one seemed more serious than previous ones. Jack had received the news that his wife Molly, who had fled to England to escape from his drinking, had finally divorced him. Teasy felt she couldn't blame the woman — Jack was fine when he was sober, but in his cups he was often spoiling for a fight. Now he took to disappearing for days on end and nobody had any idea where he was.

Then three events of extreme significance to Teasy took place.

The first occurred when she asked Dinny to go with her to a dance.

'You see, the place I used to work, a biscuit factory, they're having a dance. And some of the girls from the old days thought it would be nice if we all went. Like, a kind of a reunion.'

Dinny was very wary.

'The problem is, Teasy,' he said, 'I haven't danced for a long time. I mightn't remember the steps.'

'Sure, there's no steps nowadays — you just wriggle.'

'Ah well, that could be worse again,' said Dinny. 'The oul hip isn't the best.'

She looked at him, but didn't say what was in her mind.

'Would you give me a day or two to think about it?' asked Dinny.

A couple of days later, he told her he was sorry, but the answer would have to be no.

'Fair enough,' said Teasy.

'It's your reputation that's at stake as much as me own,' said Dinny. 'Especially with the two of us living adjacent.'

'I wonder would Stephen come,' said Teasy.

She left him staring after her with his mouth open.

The second event was the arrival of the Bishop to see Dinny. He had been a great old butty of the Monsignor's and he came to offer his sympathy and to have a bit of a chat. Teasy would have liked to meet the Bishop, but Dinny guarded him very closely and jealously, so that nobody else got the chance of having a word with His Lordship. The most that even Biddy and Miley got was a handshake. Then Dinny waved them all away and took his visitor into the cottage.

The third event took place when the visit from the Bishop was over. Teasy arrived at the cottage just in time to see his car drive away.

'Is he gone?' she asked.

'You missed him, Teasy,' said Biddy.

'Isn't that rotten!' said Teasy. 'Was he nice?'

'Oh a grand man, a grand man,' said Dinny. 'Could I have a word with you, Teasy?'

'Yeh?'

'I was thinking,' said Dinny. 'Maybe I was a bit churlish turning down your kind invitation.'

Teasy looked hard at him for a moment.

'Ah, no. It doesn't matter,' she said.

'Do you mean you have another partner?'

'No,' said Teasy. 'I was going to ask Stephen, but then I thought maybe it was a bit soon after, you know.'

'In that case,' said Dinny, 'I'd be very honoured to go with you.'

161

Teasy was almost affectedly casual.

'Yeh, all right. You mightn't like it, though.'

She stared after the Bishop's car.

'Wasn't your man very hot in his leather, running off like that!'

\*     \*     \*     \*     \*

Mary MacDermott and Dick Moran finally got married. They went to Rome for the ceremony. This was Dick's idea, because of his doubtful position in Irish civil law.

As he said himself, 'I'm going to Rome to find some exalted priest — a Bishop at least — some guy with more scarlet and gold on him than Superman. Then I'm coming back here with my little parchment and anyone who wants to say I'm not properly married is welcome to try!'

Dinny continued to be very attentive to Teasy. So was Stephen Brennan. There was an undercurrent of rivalry between the two men which made Teasy smile secretly to herself, though she didn't really admit it openly till one evening in the pub when Michelle brought it to her notice.

It was closing time and both Dinny and Stephen had been hanging on, each one showing a decided reluctance to be the first to go and leave Teasy in the company of the other. When Michelle had finally got them out the door, she turned back to Teasy.

'Aren't oul men very wicked?' she said.

'Big children,' said Teasy, 'that's all they are.'

'Of course you know you have those two fighting over *you*.'

'Yeh, isn't it great!' laughed Teasy. 'Like, to discover after all the years that you still have it.'

They were having a companionable cup of coffee together when there came a loud banging on the door. When Michelle opened it, Jack Malone fell into the bar. He was drunk.

It was Teasy who got him to bed. She knew that tiny Michelle wouldn't have the strength to handle a big man like Jack.

When she returned downstairs, she found a very worried little girl behind the bar.

'Is he all right?' asked Michelle.

'I suppose he's all right till he wakes up,'said Teasy. 'But I don't know that it's right for you to be working here.'

'He's me uncle,' said Michelle. 'I can't let him down. The problem is, how long can it last!'

'What do you mean?'

'We're in big trouble, Teasy,' said Michelle. 'We owe money every-where. If he goes on like this, we're going to lose the licence, nothing surer. Somebody's going to have to take him in hand.'

That night Teasy came to a decision.

The next day she called to see Dick Moran. She went to his own home, because she didn't want the whole town to know she intended to do business with him.

'You're a busy man, Dick,' she said. 'So I won't keep you. I have a proposition for you. It's about Jack Malone. He's going to end up in the Bankruptcy Courts, or the John of God's, one or the other.'

'Possibly both,' agreed Dick.

'If he stays in that pub he has no chance,' said Teasy. 'It's too handy for him.'

Dick shrugged.

'What can be done?'

'I want to buy the pub,' said Teasy.

She looked from Dick to Mary and back again. They were staring at her in amazement.

'I'll pay whatever it costs.'

They were still staring at her. She laughed.

'You'd want to see the two of you! You thought I hadn't a shilling, didn't you?'

Dick began to protest.

'Come on, Dick,' said Teasy. 'I'm not a complete eejit. I let people think I was on me uppers because it suited me. There was no use me arriving in Glenroe and letting everybody know what I was worth.'

Dick nodded.

'I take your point.'

'I know the two of you are too polite to ask where I got it, but I'll tell you anyway. Me sister left it to me.'

And she told them the story of Essie, the thrifty housekeeper, who had saved her pennies, invested them wisely, spent little and ended her days a very wealthy woman. And she told them how worried the Monsignor had been when he had heard just how much was involved and how he had made her promise to do nothing with the money for at least six months.

'So I put the lot in the Bank and I gave meself time to work out what I'd do with it,' she finished.

'Tell you the truth, Dick, I don't even know how much there is.'

'And now you want to buy a pub,' said Dick.'

'Not any pub. *That* pub.'

He thought a moment.

'Jack mightn't want to sell.'

'Make him an offer he can't refuse,' said Teasy.

'He can be very contrary,' said Dick.

Both Dick and Mary promised to keep the information secret, but Teasy was a good judge of the weakness of human nature. So that evening she told the story to Biddy.

'I knew Mary'd tell you, anyway,' said Teasy. 'Sure, she tells you everything. Listen, promise you'll keep it to yourself.'

'I won't even tell Miley,' said Biddy.

'Or Dinny.'

Biddy was setting the table for the evening meal. She worked in silence a moment and then said,

'Do you think it's possible that Dinny knows already?'

'I've been thinking the exact same thing meself,' said Teasy. 'Ever since the Bishop was here. It was from that day Dinny started following me around like a chihuahua.'

They both pondered the significance of this.

'Listen,' said Biddy. 'At the moment, Dinny thinks he's the only one that knows you're loaded. Well, suppose he heard that you were going to buy the pub.'

'He'd know it was all going to come out in the open,' said Teasy.

'And he might feel he'd have to make his move — fast!' said Biddy.

Teasy grinned at her.

'Wouldn't that be a rotten thing to do on him!' she said.

Biddy grinned back at her.

'Yeh, wouldn't it!'

Biddy told Dinny at the first opportunity and, as she reported back to Teasy, he feigned complete ignorance of Teasy's wealth. They had a good laugh about it. Then they settled back to see what he would do.

Jack Malone, as Dick had foretold, was proving most contrary. He steadfastly refused even to consider selling the pub. However, despite his determination to hold onto the place, he finally pulled the rug from under himself.

A couple of nights later, he arrived into the crowded pub. He was very drunk and he had a pal with him, one of the disreputable hangers-on who were always ready to help him spend his money when he was on a binge.

The whole thing started innocently enough, but Jack was at his truculent worst and reacted with violence to any suggestion from any-one to take it easy, or to mind what he was about. At first it was merely words, then the pushing started, then the fisticuffs, and finally it developed into a first-class fracas, in which even Father Devereux got his collar torn. The Gardai were called in. Sergeant Killeen gave everybody a severe talking to, before declaring the bar closed and taking Jack, for his own safety, into custody. He collared the henchman too, because he didn't like the look of him.

When everyone had left, Teasy locked the door behind them. Then she turned round and stopped in surprise. Dinny was standing before her.

'Dinny?' she said. 'Where did *you* spring from?'

'I was in the toilet,' said Dinny.

'Keeping out of trouble?'

'Ah no,' said Dinny. 'I was in the thick of it. But when I saw the Guards coming, I knew they'd clear the place. And I particularly wanted to talk to you.'

Teasy looked at him, determinedly keeping her face straight.

'You'd better come into the kitchen,' she said.

She took him inside and put the kettle on.

'We'll have a cuppa strong tea and maybe something in it,' she said.

'Aye,' said Dinny.

He sat himself at the table and looked at her appreciatively.

'You're a fine-looking woman.'

'I'm hanging on the best I can,' said Teasy, putting cups and saucers on the table.

'Sit down a minute,' said Dinny. 'I want to talk to you.'

Teasy sat and waited. Dinny got to his feet and paced nervously about.

'You're on your own, Teasy,' he said. 'Family reared, same as meself. No ties.'

She was staring at him with rapt attention.

'And I'm fond of you,' said Dinny. 'And me late brother, the Monsignor, was fond of you too.'

'He was a lovely man,' said Teasy.

'In fact,' said Dinny, pausing for emphasis, 'He sent me a message from his deathbed. To tell me to look after you.'

He stood in front of her, looking down at her bent head. Teasy was studying her fingernails.

'Now I realise that a woman like you isn't going to be short of offers,' said Dinny. 'So what I'm saying is . . . that I'd like to throw me name in the hat.'

She looked up at him, all innocent wonder.

'What are you saying, Dinny?'

'I'm proposing marriage, Teasy,' said Dinny. 'I haven't a whole lot to offer. But then nayther have you. I have the little house and a few pound put away. And the pension in a year or two.'

'And the free travel,' said Teasy.

'So I thought,' went on Dinny, 'if we were to pool our resources . . . maybe start a little business together . . . we could be snug enough.'

There was a pause.

'So there you have it,' said Dinny. 'And I'd be obliged now . . . to have your answer.'

'Will you let me get my breath,' said Teasy. 'It's not something I get asked every day, you know.'

She smiled at him.

'It isn't that I don't appreciate you asking,' she said.

'But you're saying no.' said Dinny.

'I'm not saying anything,' said Teasy, 'till I've had time to consider.'

'All right, I'll go now and leave you,' said Dinny. 'And you can inform me when you're ready.'

At the door he paused.

'I made enquiries,' he said. 'And it seems, in the month of November, they have very reasonable fares to the Canary Islands.'

When he had gone, Teasy took a few moments to let her smile out. Then she picked up the phone. When it was answered, she said,

'Hello, Biddy? Your father just left. He's hooked.'

The next day she bought the Molly Malone. Jack Malone, having been told by the Sergeant that he was certain to lose his licence, realised that he had no alternative but to sell. And he was glad, if it had to go, that it wasn't going to a stranger.

'You had us all codded,' he said to Teasy.

'Ah Jack,' said Teasy, genuinely sorry at the way things had turned out for him, ' I feel like an oul vulture, picking at your corpse.'

'Don't worry, Teasy,' said Jack, 'I'm not dead yet.'

'You don't have to get out till you're ready. Take all the time you want,' Teasy said.

'No,' said Jack. 'The sooner I get out of here the better. I'm on my way up to Dublin to book myself into a certain institution for a week or two.'

He bent and kissed Teasy on the cheek.

'Good luck, Teasy. Don't go drinking the profits,' he said. 'Cheers, Michelle.'

*　*　*　*　*

Later that evening, Teasy found Dinny in the glasshouse, tying up tomato plants.

'I promised you your answer, Dinny'.

'Will we go down to the house?' asked Dinny.

'Aren't we all right where we are!' said Teasy.

'I have the place shining,' said Dinny. 'You could ate your breakfast off the floor.'

'Well, I've had me breakfast,' said Teasy. 'So just stand there till I've said me piece. I'm afraid, Dinny, it has to be no.'

'I see,' said Dinny.

'There's something I ought to explain to you, Dinny,' said Teasy.

And she told him the whole story about Essie and the pub. He kept shaking his head in amazement.

'It's a wonder a smart man like yourself never suspected,' said Teasy, looking closely at him.

'I can tell you, Teasy,' said Dinny, innocence shining out of every pore on his face, 'it never as much as crossed me mind.'

'Yeh,' said Teasy. 'Anyway, you can see why I have to turn down your offer.'

'I don't, as a matter of fact,' said Dinny.

'Don't you see,' said Teasy. 'If I was to announce that I was buying the pub, and at the same time tell the world that we were getting engaged . . . well, there'd be people bad enough to suspect your motives.'

'But sure, I asked you before I knew you were a rich woman,' said Dinny. 'I was prepared to take you as a poor woman.'

'Ah, but they don't know that, Dinny,' said Teasy. 'There'd be talk. You could lose your friends.'

Dinny thought for a moment.

'I think I'd be willing to risk that.'

'No, Dinny,' said Teasy. 'I wouldn't put you in that position.'

She smiled sweetly at him and walked away.

The following evening Teasy told a full pub that she was the new owner. She added that she intended closing the place down for three weeks in order to have it renovated. There were cheers and congratulations all round.

The only person not one hundred percent happy was Dinny Byrne.

*　　*　　*　　*　　*

During the weeks that followed, Biddy kept Teasy informed about the movements of the two men, Dinny and Stephen. In fact, Biddy fuelled the fire herself by telling Dinny that Stephen was going to wipe his eye as far as Teasy was concerned.

Certainly, things were buzzing up at the Brennan farm. Des and Nuala had come back from England to help, bringing their little son, Max, with them. A new pitch and putt course was laid out. There was a children's playground, with a little pond and a small children's zoo. There was even talk of tennis courts. Stephen was on the move all right.

'I told Dinny,' said Biddy to Teasy, 'that there was only one explanation possible. That Stephen was planning on getting married again.'

'Ah, you didn't!'

'He pretended not to give me any heed,' said Biddy. 'But I could see it was sinking in all right.'

And, sure enough, on the day that the pub was due to reopen, Teasy caught Dinny skulking outside, trying to peer in through the window.

She rushed out into the street.

'Hey,' she called.

'Ah, Teasy . . .' Dinny began.

'Get away from there before I call the Guards,' said Teasy.

'Sure, I saw nothing.'

'You'll see it soon enough. Aren't you coming to the opening tonight?'

'I am of course,' said Dinny. 'I can hardly remember the taste of a pint.'

'I'm expecting a crowd, so you'd better come early.'

'Maybe I could come in and have a preview?'

'No, you can't,' said Teasy emphatically. 'And now I've got work to do. . . .'

'Hold on, now. Hold on,' said Dinny. 'Stay where you are and I'll give you a laugh.'

'Go on,' said Teasy. 'I could do with one.'

Dinny became very confidential.

'It's my information that Stephen Brennan is preparing to propose marriage.'

'To *me*?

'That's my information.'

Teasy smiled broadly.

'Are you serious?'

Dinny smiled back at her.

'It's as true as I'm here,' he said. 'I'm only tipping you off in advance so that you'll be able to let him down lightly.'

Teasy's smile increased in brilliance.

'Who says I'll be letting him down?'

She turned away to keep from laughing outright. Dinny stared after her, his smile completely wiped away.

That night the pub was crowded for the gala reopening. Teasy told them that the first drink was free, but after that they paid for everything they drank.

Dinny wasn't in the best of form, and his mood got even blacker when the Brennan family made their entrance later in the night. Stephen sailed in with Nuala and Des. Teasy made a point of calling out loudly.

'Ah, Stephen, me oul flower!'

'Begod, Teasy,' said Stephen, looking about him, 'it's like the Tadge Mahal!'

However, the night passed without any approaches from Stephen towards Teasy. Dinny told Biddy he was 'only biding his time' and Biddy duly reported this back to Teasy.

The following night Stephen came on his own, looking very spruced up. When he walked to the bar, Dinny made a point of joining him. Teasy hovered near them where she could overhear the conversation.

'Did you notice I got me hair cut' asked Stephen.

'I didn't, to be honest,' said Dinny.

'I went into a Unisex Barbers,' said Stephen. 'This young blondy one gave me a shampoo. Told me all about her holliers in the Canary Islands. Then a young fella with earrings starts cutting me hair. Charged me five pound fifty.'

'God save us!' said Dinny. 'Of course, five pound fifty should be nothing to a man like yourself, Stephen.'

'Oh begod, the slagging's going to start, is it?'

'Didn't I hear you were going to put in tennis courts?'

'I'm looking for permission all right,' said Stephen. 'There's a lot of things I might do. And I might do none of them. It all depends.'

'On what?' asked Dinny.

'Certain other matters,' said Stephen. 'I prefer to say nothing more for the present.'

'Do you know,' said Dinny. 'For a man that says nothing you do an awful lot of talking.'

When it was nearing closing time, Miley and Biddy took Dinny home with them. He went very reluctantly.

'What about you, Stephen?' he asked.

'Ah no, Dinny,' said Stephen. 'I . . . ah . . . wanted a private word with Teasy.'

'Oh fair enough,' said Dinny through his teeth. 'Goodnight, then. I enjoyed hearing about your haircut.'

He walked straight out of the bar without waiting for anyone else.

'Ah Teasy,' said Stephen, very pleased with himself. 'Would you give us a ball of malt for the road.'

'I heard all that,' said Teasy.

'All what?' asked Stephen innocently.

'You,' said Teasy. 'Stirring it up. Now, come on, Stephen — do you think I'm not on to you?'

Stephen sipped his whiskey.

'I don't know what you're talking about.'

'I've been watching you and I've been listening to you,' said Teasy. 'And you've been stirring it up for Dinny for the past month.'

Stephen grinned.

'Well, sure, what if I was?' he said. 'Isn't he good value for it?'

'Oh I don't mind what you do to amuse yourself,'said Teasy, 'as long as you don't drag me into it. And you can take that innocent look off your face, because you know the talk you've started. And you know it's all cod. You're an independent man and I'm an independent woman and you don't want to get married any more than I do. So why don't you stop acting the maggot and give poor Dinny a rest?'

'It was only a bit of sport,' said Stephen.

'Well, the game's over,' said Teasy. 'I've just blown the whistle.'

Stephen couldn't let it rest. A few days later he was talking to Dinny and Biddy and he told them that he wouldn't be surprised if there were 'an announcement' shortly.

Biddy told Teasy this as they were going in to early Mass.

'An announcement?' said Teasy in amazement.

'That's what he said,' said Biddy.

'He's still at it, then,' said Teasy grimly. 'I gave him a right rollicking for it, but it doesn't seem to have worked. Dinny's even stopped coming in.'

Father Devereux joined them on his way from the presbytery.

'They say this one's going to have a baby,' he grinned. 'But I don't believe a word of it.'

'I can assure you, Father . . .' said Biddy.

'Will you away out of that,' said Devereux. 'There's not a sign of you. And what about you,Teasy? When are we going to get the news of yourself?'

'Well, I hope it won't be the same as Biddy's, Father,' said Teasy.

'Oh Lord save us, no,' said Devereux. 'I was talking about you taking the plunge. There's great rumours flying about. Am I right, Biddy?'

'I never listen to rumours, Father,' said Biddy.

'Oh now, the place is buzzing,' said the priest.

He walked into the church, smiling to himself at the good of it.

'That's settles it,' said Teasy. 'One way or another Mr Brennan's got to be stopped.'

Biddy thought of a way, a very drastic way, to put a stop to Stephen's gallop. A few nights later in the pub she suggested it to Teasy.

'Ah no,' said Teasy. 'I couldn't. He doesn't deserve that.'

And she certainly wouldn't have gone any further with it had not Dinny approached her later that night.

'Excuse me,' he said, coming to the counter.

'Ah Dinny,' said Teasy. 'You're a bit of a stranger.'

Dinny spoke very quietly and seriously.

'I'd just like to be the first to congratulate you, Teasy. I know it's still hush-hush, but I understand there's to be an announcement shortly. . . .'

'Now, listen, Dinny,' said Teasy. 'Whatever Stephen said, you got it wrong.'

Dinny nodded sagely.

'I understand. I know Stephen doesn't want anything said, so . . .'

'How do you know that?' asked Teasy.

'He said it himself,' said Dinny. 'He was all for keeping it quiet and you were for telling the world.'

'Is that what he said?'

Teasy's voice was very hard.

'"It's hard to keep the women quiet",' said Dinny. 'Those were his exact words. But you can rest assured, Teasy, I'll say nothing till the white smoke comes out the chimney.'

'Thank you, Dinny.'

Looking very grim, Teasy called Biddy over.

'I've changed me mind, Biddy. Stephen deserves all that's coming to him!'

The following week an announcement appeared in the newspaper to the effect that Stephen Brennan, popular Chairman of the Glenroe Growers' Association, had announced his engagement to Mrs Teresa MacDaid of the Molly Malone Bar and Lounge, Glenroe. It took everybody by surprise, apart from Biddy and Teasy.

Stephen was absolutely stunned when he heard.

Father Devereux came into the Farm shop, his face wreathed in smiles.

'Well, Stephen, you've done it again!'

'I did what?' said Stephen as his hand was vigorously shaken.

'I have to admit you had me codded this time,' said Devereux. 'I hadn't the slightest inkling.'

'That makes two of us, Father,' said Stephen.

'Oh you're a canny man, Stephen. How in the world did you manage to keep it so quiet?'

'Father,' said Stephen, 'would you mind telling me *where* you heard whatever it was you *did* hear?'

When the priest had gone, Stephen picked up the paper and read the announcement. He stood for a long time in a state of shock. He was still barely able to function when Teasy stormed into the Farm shop.

'What do you mean, putting the like of that into the newspaper?' she hissed at him.

'Teasy, as God is my judge, it wasn't me!'

'Are you saying it was *me*?' Teasy was in full flight. 'The cheek of you! Haven't you been telling the whole of Glenroe? You told Biddy, you told Dinny.'

'They took me up wrong,' wailed Stephen.

'Listen here to me, Stephen Brennan,' said Teasy in tones of the deepest venom, 'you'll be hearing from me solicitors in due course.'

Stephen got through the day in a daze. People kept coming into the shop, shaking his hand, congratulating him, making the usual suggestive jokes and forecasts. His denials were greeted with more snide remarks, slaps on the back, and loud assertions that he was a terrible man.

The following morning he was around at the pub. He found Teasy in her overalls, cleaning the front windows.

'I was on to the paper,' said Stephen urgently. 'They want to know if they're to put in a retraction.'

'That'd only make us look even bigger eejits,' said Teasy. 'I went to see me solicitor.'

Stephen stiffened.

'He says I could sue you all right,' continued Teasy.

'But I didn't do anything!'

'That's what you say,' said Teasy. She really was enjoying herself. 'But I've got six people prepared to swear that you told them the announcement was only a formality.'

'But why would you want to go to court and drag your own name through the mud,' said Stephen.

'That was one choice,' said Teasy. 'The second one was to do nothing. He said the longer the engagement went on the more I could stick you for.'

Stephen looked appalled.

'Then there was the third suggestion,' said Teasy. 'That I should hold you to it.'

'But you don't want to get married,' said Stephen. 'You said it yourself.'

'You can get used to anything,' said Teasy.

There was a long and pregnant pause.

'Well,' said Stephen at last, 'what are you going to do?'

'I'll let you know,' said Teasy.

As she watched him go down the street, she felt slightly ashamed of herself.

'Honest to God,' she said to Biddy later. 'I'm not able for this.'

'Come on, now,' said Biddy. 'You're playing a blinder.'

'Ah, but if you'd seen him . . .' said Teasy. 'I told him I'd gone to me solicitor.'

'You didn't really go, did you?'

'I just made it up,' said Teasy. 'I'm really starting to feel sorry for him.'

'Give him another few days,' said Biddy. 'And then you can put him out of his misery.'

When she did finally send for Stephen, it was a very subdued man who presented himself at the Molly Malone.

'You took your time coming,' she said.

There was a flicker of the old Stephen.

'I'm at nobody's beck and call,' he said.

She brought him through into the kitchen, put him sitting down and poured him a glass of whiskey.

'The two of us have to decide together what we're going to do,' she said to him.

Stephen took a drink.

'I've thought the whole matter over carefully,' he said eventually. 'And I'm prepared to go through with it, for the sake of your good name.'

Teasy looked at him. She could feel a wave of sentimentality flowing over her.

'Ah no, Stephen,' she said. 'You're very considerate. But no.'

He looked at her with a glimmer of hope.

'Let's call the whole thing off,' said Teasy.

Stephen let out a long sigh.

'You're after lifting a very heavy weight off me shoulders, Teasy,' he said.

'Well, thanks very much,' said Teasy.

'You know well what I mean,' said Stephen. 'You're a fine woman. But you can't teach an old dog new tricks.'

'The old tricks would have done me,' said Teasy. 'But however . . .'

'What'll we say?' asked Stephen.

'We'll just say I changed me mind,' said Teasy.

'That's like saying you jilted me.'

'We're not saying that *you* jilted *me*, that's for sure,' said Teasy.

Stephen thought about it for some time.

'All right, then,' he said. 'You jilted me. Will we put it in the paper?'

'We'll put it about the pub,' said Teasy. 'It'll travel faster that way.'

'We don't even need to do that,' said Stephen. 'We could just tell Dinny!'

# • CHAPTER ELEVEN •

# Even Stephen

Stephen Brennan was a fair-minded man, without a trace of bigotry in his body. Live and let live, that was his motto. He had made a success of his life in the financial sense, and in any other sense you cared to mention. He owed nobody anything and he took good care that nobody owed *him* anything. He had two sons, a daughter-in-law and a grandson. He had land, greenhouses, a shop, and a leisure-complex, a modest one, but big by Glenroe standards, including a small golf course and a children's playground.

The only blemishes in his life were the death of his wife, Nancy, and the incapacity of his son, David, a victim of polio and confined to a wheelchair since his childhood. But David was an able young man for all his disability; he had graduated from the university with a degree in Commerce and was now a successful accountant. As for the death of Nancy, well, Stephen had learned to live with that.

It was hard to keep a Brennan down.

But a new problem was looming in Stephen Brennan's life. He had never liked tinkers. Travellers was what they called them nowadays, but to Stephen a tinker was a tinker, always was and always would be. But he wasn't bigoted. He hadn't anything against them as long as they stayed in their own place, wherever that might be. The further from Stephen, the better.

So he was a little disturbed when he saw the black-haired young man with the pigtail in the pub one afternoon.

'Who's your man?' Stephen asked Teasy MacDaid.

'I didn't ask him for his life-story,' said Teasy matter-of-factly. That was Teasy's fault, in Stephen's eyes. She took everything far too lightly.

'A tinker, I'd say,' said Stephen ominously.

'Traveller,' said Teasy.

'We can do without his sort around the town,' said Stephen.

'He's doing nobody any harm,' said Teasy.

'Give him an inch, though,' said Stephen. 'He'd destroy Agritourism before it got off the ground.'

Stephen was very keen on the idea of Agritourism. He had a vision of Glenroe as a centre of a thriving tourist industry based on the local farms, but particularly on his own leisure-complex. He intended building tennis courts there, just as soon as he got the necessary planning permission. He certainly didn't want any tinkers in caravans coming in and spoiling the whole thing by driving the tourists away.

He had of late taken to going about his neighbours, haranguing them on the economic desirability of Agritourism, and offering suggestions as to the part each one might play in building up the industry.

When Biddy and Miley Byrne had their first baby, Denise, Stephen had recommended that the now housebound Biddy might consider taking in paying guests for farmhouse holidays. Biddy had rejected his advice. She had no intention of being housebound. However, Miley had bought a couple of horse-drawn caravans and was in the process of refurbishing them for the summer tourist season.

'That's the way it should be,' said Stephen to Teasy. 'Everybody in the village should be involved. We'll all benefit in the long run.'

He became aware that Teasy had produced a dart board from behind the counter and was holding it up for his admiration.

'You can see I'm doing my bit for Agritourism,' she grinned at him.

'Are you codding me!'

'You're only an oul begrudger, Stephen,' said Teasy. 'Even tourists like to play darts.'

She came round from behind the counter and hung the dart board on the wall.

'Just because you don't like the game,' said Teasy.

'Oh I was very good at it when I was a nipper,' said Stephen. 'And rings. I was a great man for the rings.'

'Let's see you, then,' said Teasy.

She put some darts on top of the counter.

'I bet you couldn't even hit the wall,' she said.

Stephen sniffed at her, took a dart, aimed carefully — and hit the wall.

'I didn't mean you to take me literally,' scoffed Teasy.

'I'm just a bit short of practice, that's all,' said Stephen. 'You have to get the eye in.'

He aimed again, threw, and hit the wall again.

Father Devereux had come into the pub and paused to observe Stephen's efforts.

'You ought to try a blowpipe with that, Stephen,' he said.

'Let's see you try yourself, Father,' said Stephen. He felt he could do without the ridicule.

'Oh Lord, no,' said Devereux. 'I'd miss a stationary bus.'

'Can I get you something to drink, Father?' asked Teasy.

'Lead me not into temptation, Teasy,' said Devereux. 'I'm just in to collect a bit of tobacco. Ran out of it right in the middle of a very important letter to the County Council . . . and I find it very hard to write anything without a smoke. Ah God bless you, Teasy.'

Devereux took his tobacco and paid for it.

'Is it anything special, Father?' asked Stephen. 'The letter, I mean.'

'Just a bit of business I'm doing on behalf of the travelling people,' said Devereux.

Stephen felt his suspicions rising.

'With the County Council?'

'For a start, Stephen.'

Stephen deliberately raised his voice.

'Is it the tinkers that's above beyond Carrickvaughan? The ones that robbed Larry McDonald?'

'Now, now, Stephen,' said Devereux. 'Nothing was proven. Larry didn't identify anyone.'

Stephen looked down the bar at the dark-haired man with the pigtail. The other had his head turned away, but Stephen knew that he was listening.

'That crowd wouldn't wait around long enough to be identified,' said Stephen even more loudly. 'As far as they're concerned, prevention is better than cure. Put the run on the lot of them, that's what I say.'

The black-haired man had now put down his empty glass and was staring at Stephen. Stephen didn't meet his eye. Instead he took another dart and threw it at the dart-board. Again he missed.

Suddenly the dark-haired man strode up the bar towards Stephen. For a moment Stephen thought he was going to be attacked and he stepped back a pace. But the dark-haired man merely looked at him a moment, a little smile turning the corners of his mouth. Then he took the remaining dart from Stephen's hand and, almost without taking aim, threw it at the board. It stuck in the bull. The stranger then tipped his hat to Teasy and the priest and walked out of the bar.

He left a silence behind him. Devereux pursed his lips and moved off quietly. Teasy began busily polishing the counter. Stephen turned back to his drink.

'By God,' he said to nobody in particular.

A few days later he told the story to Dinny Byrne.

'I'm telling you, Dinny,' he said. 'It was like something out of a cowboy picture.'

'Will you listen to him!' said Teasy.

'Don't mind her, Dinny,' said Stephen. 'She was frightened out of her wits. When your man started to come at me . . .'

'He didn't "come at" you, Stephen,' interrupted Teasy. 'All he did was throw a dart at the board.'

'Oh aye,' said Stephen. 'But that was symbolic. It was a gesture against the settled community. The likes of you and me. He's the sort would destroy civilisation as we know it.'

'One black-haired scrap merchant!' said Teasy.

'Where there's one, there's two,' said Stephen. 'And where there's two, there'll soon be two hundred.'

'Give him another drink, Teasy,' said Dinny. 'And shut him up.'

'Trying to stifle the voice of reason with alcohol,' said Stephen.

He felt in his bones that there was trouble coming. The signs were on it. Caravans out on the road at Carrickvaughan, Father Devereux writing letters to the County Council, and that black fellow threatening him in the pub.

And, in one way, Stephen was right.

A short time later, at a meeting called to discuss Agritourism, Father Devereux made an announcement. The County Council had bought a site in Glenroe for new houses and the plan was that some of these would go to travellers who wished to be housed. The meeting immediately forgot about Agritourism and deteriorated into arguments for and against the Council project.

Stephen was incensed. He had put in a bid for that particular site himself, though that wasn't the main cause of his anger. It was the idea that tinkers should be settled in Glenroe which really upset him. He had visions of hundreds of black-haired men with pigtails walking the streets of the village, throwing litter about the place and generally causing trouble.

He immediately started a campaign against the plan. One of his strongest allies was Mynah Timlin, a woman with a large family and an ailing husband. Mynah was an incurable gossip, who did cleaning jobs around the village for people like Dick Moran and Teasy MacDaid. She was always willing to stir up trouble whenever she could. But there were others too, who felt like Stephen. Solid citizens. People who were genuinely afraid that the value of their property would go down with a lot of scrap merchants living up the road.

Even Dick Moran.

Stephen knew that Dick rarely did anything without expecting something in return. But there was that bit in the Bible about making friends of the mammon of iniquity and Stephen was prepared to go along with anything which might help to keep the travellers out of Glenroe. When Dick announced that he had an alternative site, which the Council might be persuaded to buy for the project, Stephen welcomed the idea. Even though he knew that Grallagh was a bit of near-bogland, there was nothing to prevent the Council draining it and making it suitable.

He went about collecting names for a petition. He knocked on doors, talked to people, used all the arguments he could to get people to sign, and eventually came up with a sizeable list.

When he spoke to Father Devereux about it, he found that the priest wasn't against an alternative site, but only if the travellers were happy with it. To this end, Stephen agreed to meet a representative of the travellers. He wasn't so happy, however, when he found out that the representative was none other than Blackie Connors, the dart-throwing man with the pigtail.

Stephen went to find Mick Killeen. Mick had lately retired from the Garda Siochana. He had been a popular and relatively easy-going sergeant and was now a hackney driver.

'Mick,' said Stephen. 'Are you busy?'

'I never refuse a customer,' said Killeen.

'Ah no,' said Stephen. 'All I want is a bit of help. I'm having a meeting with that fella Connors from the camp site in Carrickvaughan. I was wondering if you'd like to come along with me.'

'Me?'

'You see,' said Stephen, 'the first time I met him we didn't exactly hit it off. He sort of threatened me.'

'That's a job for the Gardai,' said Killeen. 'I've hung up my baton.'

'All I want is a friend,' said Stephen. 'With a bit of muscle.'

'A sort of a minder, is it?'

'I just think your presence would have a . . . calming influence on the proceedings,' said Stephen.

The next day Stephen, with Killeen in attendance, was waiting in the pub when Blackie Connors entered. Stephen immediately stood up, doing his best to be friendly and reassuring.

'Ah yes,' he said. 'It's Blackie Connors, I presume.'

'Only me friends call me Blackie,' said Blackie. He added, after a pause, 'Mr Brennan.'

He was staring at Killeen.

'What's he doing here?' he asked.

'He's a friend of mine,' said Stephen.

'He's a Guard,' said Blackie.

Stephen tried to make a joke.

'Oh I don't mind who I make friends with,' he said.

'Nobody said anything about a Guard,' said Blackie. 'I'm not staying if he's here.'

Killeen stood up.

'I'd better be on my way so, Stephen,' he said.

'Stay where you are, Mick,' said Stephen.

'Right,' said Blackie.

He turned away and started towards the door.

'Listen,' Stephen called after him. 'I want to talk to you about the site below in Grallagh.'

Blackie paused and turned around.

'I'm doing no talking while he's here,' he said. 'But I'll say this. Grallagh is only fit for ducks. And my people are going to no bogland. We'll stay in Glenroe.'

'There's a lot in Glenroe think different,' said Stephen.

'Right,' said Blackie. 'Let them think what they want.'

He walked out of the pub. Killeen turned to Stephen.

'You lost that battle, Stephen,' he said.

'Maybe so,' said Stephen grimly. 'But I haven't lost the war.'

*     *     *     *     *

Despite Stephen's best efforts, however, which included taking his list of names to the County Manager, the building of the houses went ahead. True, the travellers did disappear for a while. Stephen went about informing everybody that that was the way of it with tinkers — they pulled up stakes and took off when the mood hit them. It was useless offering them houses; they just wouldn't stay in them. And they were happier on the road. If God had meant them to live in houses, he wouldn't have provided them with caravans and horses and vans.

However, he was a pragmatic man. When he recognised the inevitability of the housing project, he ceased his objection to it. He even came around to wishing the tinkers well, wherever they had got themselves to, but he still couldn't bring himself to believe that they'd ever settle down in a village like normal people.

Then one day the caravans arrived back to Carrickvaughan. To Stephen's eyes there were children and horses everywhere. He felt plagued by horses. They grazed along the side of the road and he hated the sight of them. They put him in bad humour.

And they were responsible for what happened

He was out one night with his shotgun, looking for rabbits. As he walked down the fairway of his golf-course, he saw the form of a horse looming out of the mist. The animal was grazing on the seventh green, pulling at the grass, digging its large hooves into the turf. In a fit of rage, Stephen raised the gun and fired a shot in front of the animal. It was only when the smoke had cleared that he saw a second horse stretched on the ground.

Next day he found out that the horses had nothing to do with the travellers. They belonged to Miley Byrne, who used them for his horse-drawn holiday caravans. There were recriminations and arguments and Stephen had to put his hand in his pocket and fork out compensation to Miley.

So he was in no mood for jokes when four travellers came into his shop one day soon after, four skittish young men led by Blackie Connors. Blackie picked up an apple.

'Are you buying that?' asked Stephen sharply.

Blackie put down the apple.

'No,' he said. 'We'll take a bag.'

He tore the plastic bag and handed the apples to his friends. He grinned at Stephen.

'I hear you shot a horse.'

'I've nothing to say about it,' said Stephen.

'Whose horse was it?' asked Blackie.

'It wasn't yours,' said Stephen. 'That's all should concern you.'

'Sure, I've no horses now,' said Blackie. 'Was it a traveller's horse?'

'I believe it was Miley Byrne's,' said Stephen.

He wished they'd get out of his shop and leave him alone.

'I sold him that horse,' said Blackie. 'Last Christmas. I'd say Miley's vexed.'

He was smiling all the time. Stephen took the grin as an insult.

'Was there anything else you wanted?'

'You're a tough man all the same,' said Blackie. 'Shooting the oul horse.'

'If there's nothing else you want,' snapped Stephen, 'you can take yourselves off.'

'We thought we'd have a game of golf,' said Blackie, still smiling at him.

'Did you now!' said Stephen. 'Well, you won't be playing it here.'

Blackie's smile faded.

'We have the money,' he said.

'It isn't the money.'

'What is it, then?'

Stephen pointed to a large notice on the wall behind him.

'If you can read that,' he said. 'It says "The Management reserves the right to . . ."'

'I can read,' said Blackie. 'Are you refusing us?'

'I am.'

'Why?'

'I don't have to give you any explanations,' said Stephen. 'So off you go.'

The other travellers looked at Blackie, waiting for his lead. There was a pause. For a moment Stephen thought that they were going to attack him and he stiffened. But Blackie merely shrugged.

'Right,' he said. 'We won't give any trouble. Come on, lads.'

He turned at the door.

'But we'll be back.'

The next morning at breakfast, Stephen's daughter-in-law, Nuala, spoke to him about the incident.

'I heard about Blackie,' she said. 'Why did you turn him away?'

'I can turn away whoever I want,' said Stephen.

'Sure you can,' said Nuala. 'If you have a reason.'

'Oh I had a reason all right,' said Stephen. 'But I don't see what business it is of yours.'

'Did Father Devereux not tell you that he's appointed a representative for the travellers?' said Nuala.

'He can appoint anyone he wants,' said Stephen. 'They'll all get the same answer.'

'I'm the representative, Stephen,' said Nuala.

Stephen stared at her.

'Well, dammit,' he said. 'Why do you always want to go against me!'

'Look,' said Nuala, 'all I'm doing is asking you a question. Why don't you let them play?'

But Stephen wasn't prepared to discuss the matter.

'It's between them and me. You stay out of it.'

He got up and left the room.

But later that same day he was approached by Father Devereux himself.

'It's not my place to take sides, Stephen,' said the priest. 'But would you not be the decent man I know you to be and let the lads come in and play a game? Sure, what possible harm could they do?'

'They could only wreck the place,' said Stephen. 'What do the likes of them know about the niceties of the game? Like replacing divots?'

'Is that not just a matter of a word in their ear?'

'If I let one in, isn't he going to bring his whole seed, breed and generation in after him!'

'I can only say I'm surprised at you, Stephen,' said Devereux.

'And I'm surprised at you, Father,' said Stephen hotly. 'Getting Nuala to take sides against her own family. I thought the clergy was supposed to *support* the family!'

Devereux looked at him a moment, letting him cool down.

Then he said, 'It's my job to make lads like Blackie feel part of the community. I'm asking you, Stephen, as a personal favour, to give them a chance.'

Stephen looked away for a moment.

'All right, Father,' he said finally. 'If you put it like that.'

Devereux clapped him on the shoulder.

'Good man, Stephen,' he said. 'I never doubted you!'

And so it was that a couple of days later Blackie and his friends arrived back in Stephen's shop. Stephen was serving a customer at the time, but he kept a suspicious eye on the travellers till the customer had left.

'We'd like to have a go at the golf,' said Blackie.

Stephen hesitated. Then he turned away to get the clubs. Behind him he could hear the faint sound of a chuckle.

'We'll take a bag of apples too,' said Blackie.

He took a bag of apples off the counter. As he opened it, the apples spilled out onto the ground. There was more giggling from the travellers as they bent to retrieve them.

Stephen turned round, stony-faced, with the eight clubs in his hand.

'That's six pound for the round, and seventy pence for the apples,' he said.

He waited while Blackie fished in his pocket and brought out the money.

'And forty pound deposit,' said Stephen.

'What?'

'Eight clubs. Five pound deposit on each club. That's forty pound,' he said.

Blackie looked at him incredulously.

'Are you joking?'

'That's the terms,' said Stephen adamantly.

'Will you take a cheque?' asked Blackie.

'A travellers' cheque,' said one of his friends.

They all laughed.

'No,' said Stephen. 'And something else I won't take. People like you coming in here thinking I'm good for a laugh. I won't take that either.'

'Nobody was laughing at you,' said Blackie.

'Do you want to play, or don't you?'

'We haven't got forty pound,' said Blackie.

'Fair enough,' said Stephen. 'Come back when you have.'

He put the clubs away. Blackie looked stonily at him for a moment. Then he turned and led his companions out of the shop.

Stephen hummed a little tune to himself as he resumed serving his real customers. He felt he had done rather well, broken no promises to Father Devereux, and protected his own property at the same time.

When, next day, he saw the picket outside his gate, he couldn't believe his eyes. There they were, parading around in a circle — his own daughter-in-law, Nuala, his grandson, little Max, Blackie and his three mates, and a couple of travelling women.

The placards read, 'Travellers' Rights, No Dogs, No Blacks, No Tinkers, Apartheid Irish Style,' and other insulting messages.

As he stared at this ugly sight, Stephen was joined by his son, Des, who was as incensed as he was himself.

'How can you picket your own house?' Des shouted at his wife.

'I'm not picketing the house,' Nuala shouted back. 'I'm picketing the golf-course.'

'Well, begod, I'll picket the house,' said Stephen angrily. 'I won't let you next or near it!'

'Go ahead,' said Nuala. 'I lived before I knew you!'

'Such carry on,' said Stephen. 'In front of the child.'

Nuala looked down at her son.

'Max,' she said, 'are you enjoying yourself?'

There was no doubt in the world that Max was having a wonderful time. He had a lollipop to eat and a lot of friendly people to play with him.

'Listen, Nuala,' said Des. 'I'm saying this for the last time. Come home!'

'No,' said Nuala very calmly. 'Start treating people like human beings and we can *all* go home.'

Stephen walked up to her.

'What do you mean by that, Miss?'

'Why didn't you let them play?'

'I never stopped them playing,' said Stephen. 'They can play all they want.'

'If they pay forty pounds!'

'That's the deposit on the clubs,' said Stephen. 'I'm entitled to charge it.'

'You don't charge other people,' said Nuala.

'I do so.'

'Who?'

'People I don't trust,' said Stephen triumphantly.

Nuala turned to the travellers.

'You heard that? OK. Keep moving!'

The picket resumed the march around the road.

'Nuala,' said Des. 'I'm warning you! For the last time!'

'Ah sure, you're only wasting your breath,' said Stephen. 'She's determined to make a show of us all!'

'We're only exercising our democratic rights,' Nuala shouted across at them.

Stephen stamped back into his shop. He was angry and very brusque with those customers who came in and asked him what was going on outside. That slip of a girl was always getting at him! But there was no way he was going to give in! That wasn't the style of the Brennans at all!

He was up the ladder, fixing his stock, when he heard some people come in behind him. He turned and stared at them. Then he slowly came down the ladder.

'What do you want *now*?' he asked.

It was Blackie and his three companions.

'We'd like to have a go at the golf,' he said.

There was a long pause as Stephen contemplated them.

'I'll say one thing for you,' he said at length. 'You have neck.'

'Mr Brennan,' said Blackie in a conciliatory tone, 'we're sorry about the trouble and the bad feeling. But there's two sides.'

'There was never any bad feeling on my side,' said Stephen.

'That's good to hear,' said Blackie.

'Not one iota,' said Stephen, beginning to believe his own assertions. 'You're welcome to play any time you want. As long as you're pre-pared to pay ten pound a man deposit on the clubs.'

'Ah well, you see,' said Blackie, 'that won't come into it. We have our own.'

At that, the travellers produced two clubs apiece from behind their backs. Stephen looked at the clubs. Then he looked at the travellers, waiting for the suggestion of a smirk. But they were all very solemn-faced.

'Where'd you get them?' he asked.

'That's the great thing about travellers, Mr Brennan,' said Blackie. 'They're great at the dealing. There's not much they can't put their hands on.'

'It was yourself that said it,' said Stephen. He turned and began to rummage in a drawer.

'What do you say, Mr Brennan?' asked Blackie.

'Give us six pound,' said Stephen.

He produced a book of tickets and pulled out four. Blackie gave him six pounds.

'You want balls,' Stephen said, turning to get them.

'We've those as well,' said Blackie. He took some balls from his pocket and showed them.

Stephen nodded. He could recognise a defeat when he saw it.

'Right,' he said. 'Away you go.'

They turned to go. Then Blackie paused and picked up a bag of apples.

'Oh here . . .' he began.

'Go on,' said Stephen. 'I'll throw those in.'

Blackie stared at him in surprise.

'Thanks, Mr Brennan.'

'And don't throw the stumps in the bunkers,' said Stephen.